A Beam *of* Hope

Trophies of Grace Series

BOOK 1

Betty J Hassler

This is a work of fiction. All of the characters, names, incidents, and dialogue in this novel are the products of the author's imagination or are used fictionally.

WestBow Press books may be ordered through booksellers or by contacting:

WestBow Press
A Division of Thomas Nelson & Zondervan
1663 Liberty Drive
Bloomington, IN 47403
www.westbowpress.com
844-714-3454

ISBN: 978-1-6642-6706-0 (sc)
ISBN: 978-1-6642-6705-3 (hc)
ISBN: 978-1-6642-6707-7 (e)

Library of Congress Control Number: 2022909142

Print information available on the last page.

WestBow Press rev. date: 06/03/2022

To caring, mature believers who taught me so much
about intergenerational family dynamics
and the wisdom of the elderly.

ACKNOWLEDGMENTS

Walking my dog through my Nashville, Tennessee, neighborhood was an everyday occurrence. But on this particular day, a fictional story began forming as I traveled the familiar turf. Even the name of the main character jumped to mind. As more and more of the story unfolded, I could only assume I should begin typing.

After all, I was an editor for a Christian publisher at the time and had been writing novels since I learned to read and write. Alas, I don't know what happened to those masterpieces of juvenile fiction. But I do know that Layton Brooks and the ensuing characters in *A Beam of Hope* finally found their way into print. Thank you to WestBow Press for making this reiteration of the dream come true. To my editors, a special word of gratitude. Oh, the things I would have missed if it weren't for your careful inspection!

I would like to thank you, my readers, for your interest. May you be encouraged to share your beam of hope with others to remind you that God is up to something in your life.

Always be ready to offer a defense, humbly and respectfully, when someone asks why you live in hope. (1 Peter 3:15 The Voice New Testament)

I'd also like to thank my long-suffering husband, Sim, for reading every word of the manuscript, asking penetrating questions, telling me when he felt lost in the maze of characters and plot, and, especially, shedding a tear in all the right places.

I thank God for giving me the vision for this series, Trophies of Grace. I pray it will demonstrate through the lives of everyday people how You lavish Your children with hope, faith, mercy, and love. May His grace overflow as you read.

PROLOGUE

Fall 1993

Layton Brooks stood in the doorway of his man cave. Years ago, he'd playfully posted a commercial *Keep Out* sign on the door. However, a mischievous nine-year-old had scratched through it with a big red X. With large letters, she'd carefully printed, *Come on In*.

Now the little girl was grown and away at college. However, the invitation stood. Inside, friends and family had taken their places around the imposing trophy case on the back wall between two windows. The glass shelves contained memories that would outlive him.

On the top shelves stood his most prized possessions. Each trophy had been engraved with a person's name, date, and quality he or she represented. He'd presented the trophies in person or, in one case, in absentia. These heroes of faith had been his spiritual mentors. People such as Myra Norwell, who demonstrated peace in her illness. How about Brianne's endurance when she'd received a similar diagnosis?

Layton ambled toward his recliner, coffee cup in hand, eyes still on the trophy case. When the time came to unveil a new trophy, he'd presented it to those gathered to "build faith muscles," as he put it. Always tears and hugs followed the brief ceremony.

The idea had come from Meme Dyer, his daughter Brianne's grandmother. Once, as they were saying their goodbyes at the Nashville airport, Meme had affirmed that God's good purposes in Brianne's illness would be a trophy of His grace.

Back home from the airport, Layton had looked again at the wooden cabinet poised against the wall of his man cave. Hmm, he'd mused, a trophy of God's grace. A trophy case to display God's grace! Suddenly, the piece of furniture took on a whole new meaning:

Grace is God's way of treating us as though we are deserving of His blessings—although, of course, we're not.

Meme's optimism had been the inspiration for the trophy Layton had awarded her—a trophy for hope. Her daughter Amy had been the one to label her mother a beam of hope in their darkest hours.

Layton let out a long, satisfied sigh. Settling his lanky frame into his well-worn recliner, he placed the coffee cup on the end table. Memories flooded him. True, life would have been very different if Brianne's illness had led to another conclusion. Maybe life would have been less complicated. But so much less rewarding. That had been many years ago.

Too bad the story of how it all came about had begun on such a dismal note. He frowned, recalling that foggy morning in 1979 when he'd set out for Nashville—the last place on earth he wanted to be.

Spring 1979

Layton Brooks turned his car off I-95 onto the Pennsylvania turnpike and headed west. Light rain peppered his windshield. He knew flying would have made more sense. A couple of hours, and he'd be in Nashville. But Layton wasn't ready to be there, and he couldn't think of another way to delay the inevitable.

Too soon he'd have to look into the piercing blue eyes of the woman he'd loved—probably still loved—on the arm of another man. More troubling, his precious four-year-old daughter, Brianne, would be lying in a hospital bed awaiting cancer surgery. Together, the prospect seemed overwhelming.

He hid his emotions well. Perhaps too well. At some point, his anger would no doubt boil to the surface and explode over whoever was unfortunate enough to be present.

Layton glanced at his wristwatch. The weekend traffic was light. With any luck, he could make it to Cincinnati tonight and on into Nashville tomorrow. He signaled to pass a slow-moving RV. It was going to be a long trip. Or maybe too short. He wasn't sure yet.

The late-afternoon sun beat on his back. Layton felt glued to the seat. He stretched his lanky frame and yawned. The drive had been uneventful except for a few speeding drivers weaving between the 18-wheelers.

Thinking about Brianne helped the hours creep forward. Always flitting around like a butterfly, Brianne was the most energetic three—oops—four-year-old girl he knew. He'd missed her fourth birthday party. At that thought, he tousled his blondish-brown hair.

In fact, he hadn't seen her since Christmas and then only for two days. What do you do with a three-year-old when you're living out of a motel room? he wondered for the umpteenth time. Taking her back and forth to a house he'd once owned and lived in felt too awkward.

Nothing seemed fair, least of all Brianne's diagnosis. She'd just started gymnastics in January. Somehow the thought of her being admitted to a hospital seemed bizarre. He leaned his long frame toward the steering wheel to dry out the back of his shirt.

Since his move to New Jersey, he'd made it a point to keep up with her daily experiences as often as possible. Phone conversations with her were almost like talking to a grown-up.

"Why didn't you answer the phone, Daddy? I tried to call you."

"I've been unloading groceries, Kitten."

"Meow." Brianne often made a cat sound when he called her Kitten. He wasn't quite sure why he did that. A habit from somewhere. He didn't even particularly like cats.

"What did you buy at the store?"

"Lots of frozen stuff. I had to put it in the freezer."

"Oh." She paused. "Mommy made cookies today, Daddy. Would you like a cookie?"

"Sure would." He'd made chewing sounds. "That tasted yummy."

In these lighthearted moments, Brianne offered him other things to eat—a turtle, a dinosaur, a flower—whatever else she could imagine. He'd pretend to eat them all, to her amusement. She always ended their phone conversation with "I miss you, Daddy."

"I miss you too," he'd reply. "I love you."

Remembering brought an unexpected lump to his throat. Maybe a cup of strong coffee would help. He exited I-71 and turned into the parking lot of the first restaurant he spotted. *Might as well eat dinner too. Only another hour or so to Cincinnati.*

❧

Back in the car, Layton continued replaying past conversations with Brianne. *Strange*, he mused. Most of her life, he'd spent weekdays traveling on business. Their brief early-evening visits occurred by phone from a motel room.

After he filed for divorce, Layton accepted a position in his company's New York City home office. Although the commute to and from his condo in New Jersey left little time in his day, at least he was home at night. Now that he didn't travel much, he had no family to come home to.

At least he could still call her. Because of the change from eastern to central time zone in Nashville, he had an extra hour to catch his daughter before bedtime. Brianne would report on her day as if she were keeping a diary. "Taylor came to my house. Mommy kept her so her daddy could go to work."

"You and Taylor are getting to be good friends. How old is she?"

"She's five, Daddy. She can count to a hundred and swing way up high. We played picnic."

"Who came to the picnic, Kitten?"

"Meow. You, Daddy. Don't you remember? You sat right by me."

"What did I have to eat?"

"A hot dog with mus-ter and relish. The way you like it."

"Mustard, huh?"

"Yes, and tomorrow we're going to the zoo."

Painful memories consumed his review of Brianne's musings. "Who's that in the background?"

"Oh, that's Mr. Stephen, Taylor's dad. They ate dinner with us. Taylor threw up."

"Your mom's not that bad a cook," Layton teased.

"No, no. Mommy says she's coming down with something."

"Where's her mom?"

"She died, Daddy. Don't you remember?"

At the thought of that last conversation, Layton had no interest in remembering phone calls.

ஒ

The motel room looked serviceable, if not up to his usual business expense trip standards. Layton unpacked the few things he required for the night and stretched out on the bed to call his ex-wife, Amy. *As if everything isn't already hard enough*, he thought.

Amy answered on the first ring. "Layton, where are you?"

"Hello to you too."

"I'm sorry. I'm just so ready for you to get here."

"I wish you'd been ready a year ago," he answered testily, immediately sorry for his words.

"Please, not now. Not when Brianne needs us so much."

After a long pause, he managed to say, "I'm in Cincinnati. I should be in Nashville by midafternoon tomorrow. Is Brianne asleep?"

"Unfortunately, no." Layton could hear the tension in her voice. He'd better tread lightly.

"How is she?" he asked reluctantly, hoping Amy wouldn't tell him more than he was prepared to hear.

"Actually, she's excited about going into the hospital. That's why I can't get her to sleep. She wants to take the doctor's kit you sent with her tomorrow."

Layton chuckled. So like Brianne to think she'd be in charge of the operation. "I'll check in at my hotel and then come straight to the hospital."

"Okay. Call me when you're ready to leave tomorrow."

"Why? I'll see you—"

"Something might come up," she interrupted. "I just want to know you're on your way."

"No problem."

"Talk to you then. And thanks for coming."

After she hung up, Layton sat the phone on its hook and stretched out on the bed. Tears welled in his eyes. Fighting to keep them back, he almost uttered a prayer for his Kitten—before he remembered he didn't believe in prayer anymore.

Layton stood outside the hospital room for what seemed an eternity. He'd probably still be standing there if a nurse hadn't brushed by him on her way into Brianne's room. The motion caught Amy's attention. She ran to him and threw her arms around him. Layton stood there woodenly. Finally, he let his arms drop like an umbrella around his ex-wife. Not quite a hug but an acknowledgment of their mutual pain.

"Brianne's been asking for you." Amy led him inside the room.

Layton stood there, looking bewildered, not sure what to do next. Brianne napped peacefully. She looked so small in that big bed. Sensing his confusion, Amy guided him to the chair by the bed.

"She just dropped off to sleep. The doctor came by this morning. We've got one of the best pediatric cancer specialists in the country, and Vanderbilt Hospital is among the top. Brianne is very fortunate."

Layton couldn't quite figure how his tiny daughter with a cancerous tumor ranked among the fortunate. He let the comment pass. "We can talk about all of that later. Right now, why don't you take a break? You look tired," he concluded, without much tact.

True, Amy had swollen eyes and smudged eye makeup—had she been crying?—and tousled red hair. But nothing could make her look less than breathtakingly beautiful. In her blue jeans and sweater, she looked like the college coed he'd fallen in love with years ago. He shifted his eyes away from her brilliant blue ones. "Go on now. Get some lunch."

She agreed reluctantly and grabbed her purse. "I'll run home for a while if you don't mind. I left the place in a mess."

"Take your time. I'm not going anywhere." Truth be told, Layton would rather be anywhere else on earth. But he wasn't going anywhere at all. Not when his only child—his four-year-old Kitten—lay sleeping in a hospital bed.

⁂

After Amy left, Layton dozed, one ear cocked in case Brianne awoke. He hadn't slept well the night before. In fact, not since the surgery had been scheduled and he knew he'd return to Nashville. Strange. He'd grown up here and thought he loved every inch of the place. Now it seemed eons ago. Finally, he fell into a deep sleep. In his dream, he and his daughter were playing in the living room with her toy cash register. "That'll be twenty- ninety forty dollars and nine cents," Brianne told him. "Please come again."

She handed him a stuffed giraffe, two plastic tomatoes, and a purple ring off a ring-toss pole.

That peaceful scene disappeared, replaced by the terror of her cancer. "Daddy, don't let it get me. Daddy! Daddy!" Brianne screamed as she ran into the gnarled thicket of Layton's dream. The twisted branches grabbed at her with skeletal fingers. Layton couldn't move a muscle to save his little girl. All he could do was scream along with her.

⁂

"Daddy! Daddy!"

Layton's eyes snapped open. Half-awake, he expected to see the face of a horrified child. Instead, he looked into the dancing blue eyes of his strawberry-blonde daughter, sitting up in her oversized hospital bed.

"Daddy, you're here! You said you were going to come." Her voice chased away his nightmare and replaced it with a tremendous sense of relief. He reached for her, and they hugged for a long time. "Mommy said when I get home, you'll stay with me. I can ride my bike now without the training wheels. Do you want to see me ride my bike?"

"I sure do, Kitten."

"Meow," she sang out playfully. They grinned at each other.

"Mommy said the doctors are going to make me all better. God told her. God told me too. We say our prayers every night before I go to bed."

Oh no, here it comes, Layton thought. *The God talk. From her mother, no less. The one fooling around on me with Taylor's dad.* He didn't even know Stephen's last name. Frustrated, Layton ran his fingers through his short brown hair.

If prayer hadn't worked for him, why it would work for Amy? He had been about as good a Christian as he knew. The thought of his hypocritical wife beseeching God with any degree of success stirred his frustration.

Now that Amy had become a believer, suddenly the past didn't seem to matter to her. Besides, what could Amy say in a prayer that God hadn't already heard from her own mother and father? At least Jan and Phil Dyer were sincere in their faith.

The rest of the afternoon, when the nurses weren't sticking and poking their little patient, Layton and Brianne colored pictures and read stories. Tests and more tests interrupted their play. Then Brianne was wheeled to the MRI for a final look at the tumor.

And where is Amy? His rumbling stomach reminded him he'd forgotten to eat lunch.

❧

Shortly after Amy returned, the doctor came in. Amy introduced him to Dr. Holt, a middle-aged woman with a ready smile and firm handshake. Layton liked her at once. Obviously, his daughter felt the same way.

After the preliminaries, the doctor got to the point. "Tomorrow we'll be in surgery for about two hours. A patient representative will bring you news from the operating room every half hour or so. We plan to excise the entire tumor. Then we'll take samples from the surrounding tissue. We don't think the cancer has spread, but we won't know until we get lab results."

Layton glanced at Amy's anxious face, hoping for some sign of comfort.

Dr. Holt continued, "Depending on her pain level, Brianne will be home in a day or so. When she's strong enough, we'll resume further treatment if it proves necessary."

"We're so glad she's in your hands, Dr. Holt. I've heard so many good things about you," Amy said. "We're praying for a miracle."

Layton stiffened. "I'm sure your fine surgical skills will be more than adequate," he countered.

"Oh, I like all the help I can get," Dr. Holt replied with a smile. "Pray all you want." With that, she shook their hands and turned back to Brianne.

"Brianne, do you have any questions?"

"When will I get to eat?"

The doctor laughed and spent the next few minutes explaining in simple language what would happen after surgery.

Layton felt lightheaded. He excused himself and headed toward the cafeteria. *How am I going to get through this?* he wondered. He had a lot of confidence in modern medicine but not much confidence that prayer would make a difference.

Layton had drunk all the coffee his nervous system could take. The patient rep had been in to say the doctor had started the surgery. Amy led a heartfelt, tender prayer for their daughter while he gritted his teeth. He said a loud "Amen" to punctuate the end of the subject.

In the grogginess of a fairly sleepless night, Layton hadn't thought much about what would happen during the hours while he and Amy awaited the outcome of Brianne's surgery. He didn't have to wonder long. Within minutes, friends started arriving, including couples they had known during their marriage.

At first, Layton stood around, lamely listening more than talking. What should he say? "Welcome to Traumaville. So nice of you to come. How's it going?" Although in one sense he felt glad to see them, each familiar face might as well have been a knife prick to the father who was no longer married to the patient's mother. He felt drained by the well-meaning small talk. Trapped inside his body, his voice wanted to scream, "I am not ok! Nothing is right here!"

He wished for his older brother's calming presence. Kyle would know what to do and say. He'd always taken care of Layton in a tight spot. Too bad Kyle's military tour had been extended. With his dad's premature death and his mother's Alzheimer's, Layton had no immediate family to turn to. Amy was an only child, and her parents were out of the country. Besides, Layton wasn't exactly close to them.

Standing there in the circle of former friends and his ex-wife, he felt utterly alone and helpless to change his circumstances.

❧

Layton hadn't realized he was lost in thought until the elevator bell rang outside the waiting room. He heard a familiar voice approaching. Rev. Frank Norwell—his pastor for all of his thirty years—had baptized, married, and then comforted Layton during the divorce. He stopped to speak to hospital staff with the easy familiarity of a frequent visitor.

His hair had turned salt-and-pepper gray, but his trim frame spoke to his intense love of tennis. Layton's dad and he had played doubles tournaments. What little emotional control Layton had left dissolved, and he excused himself to the men's restroom. Moments later, when he emerged with a freshly washed face, his minister stood waiting for him.

"Layton, it's good to see you. I'm so sorry about Brianne. How is she?"

Layton struggled to appear strong. "Thanks for coming, Pastor Frank. Brianne's still in surgery, but I know she's going to be all right. She's a tough little girl."

They talked for several minutes while Layton paced up and down the hallway, giving the minister a workout. Finally settling in an armchair, he found himself cornered when Pastor Frank brought up the subject he had been trying so hard to avoid.

"How are things between you and God?

When the patient rep appeared in the doorway, Layton hastily exited the chair, leaving Pastor Frank's question hanging in midair. He and Amy reached the smiling lady almost at the same moment, bumping shoulders. "Dr. Holt wants you to know that the surgery went well. Brianne is stable, and her vital signs are strong. The doctor will be closing the incision and out to talk with you in a half hour or so."

Amy collapsed in tears, the absolutely last reaction Layton expected. *Did I miss something? I thought everything went great.*

Amy's best friend, Beth Braxton, offered to get her something to eat. Amy nodded, and Beth headed to the cafeteria. Layton thought that sounded like a great idea. Suddenly, he could eat a cow. "I'll grab something too."

"May I go with you?" Pastor Frank asked. Layton couldn't think of a polite way to refuse his request.

Settled in a booth with their snacks, the minister bowed his head. "Lord, bless this food we are about to eat. I thank You that little Brianne made it through the surgery well. I praise You for the skilled hands of the surgical staff and for the way You made our bodies to heal. I pray for Brianne's parents as they talk with the doctor. Guide each decision, and may Your will be done."

Layton had actually been listening until that last sentence. Anger welled inside again. *God's will? I want my will. I stopped praying for God's will when I signed the divorce papers.*

❧

Layton found it fairly easy to turn the conversation with Pastor Frank away from God and toward Vanderbilt University football. "Did you see the bowl game? What about that field goal that sealed the win in the fourth quarter? Go Commodores!"

Pastor Frank beamed with pride. He replayed the pass interception in the last few minutes that set up the kick. "I wish your dad could have seen that game." Pastor Frank enjoyed a bite of cinnamon roll. "I've never seen a more intense Vandy fan than Al Brooks. In fact, I think I heard Al shouting from heaven when the game buzzer sounded."

Layton's lips tightened. His pastor's comment reminded him that his sole comfort in his dad's sudden death had been the knowledge that he was in heaven, and Layton would see him again someday. He'd died in his late fifties, before old age eased the transition.

Layton had been taught that bad things happen to good people. He'd made his peace with God. Then two years later, he got the news about his mother. His dad's death had rocked his boat, but the news of his mother's early onset of Alzheimer's had splintered the bow.

Now his thoughts wandered completely away from the hospital cafeteria to a question that had plagued him for years. Why would a good God allow a woman who had done nothing but serve other people all her life to have to struggle with such a horrible disease? It certainly didn't seem fair or right.

He'd felt fortunate that Claire Brooks got to meet her granddaughter Brianne before she had to give up living alone. As her health declined, she had inspired him with her courage. Claire thanked God for everything good that came her way, even the opening to get into one of the best Alzheimer's care facilities in the city.

However, he'd pretty much stopped seeing his mother by the time of the divorce. She didn't recognize Brianne, and occasionally, in Claire's mind, Layton would be Kyle or his dad. The experience caused too much pain and seemed pointless. After all, she wouldn't remember that Layton had come. Better to leave the good memories intact.

Layton felt the slow burn of his anger rising from a deep pool within. Without any immediate family around to share his sorrow, he felt abandoned. He'd tried to be a good husband and father. He'd supported his family well through hard work and long hours. What did he have to show for it?

"Layton." When Pastor Frank called his name, he returned to the reality of the hospital cafeteria. The minister began collecting dishes. "How about letting me clean off the table while you get back upstairs? I've got an appointment at the office in about fifteen minutes."

"Sure, Pastor Frank. Thanks." He looked at his half-eaten food. "I guess I wasn't hungry after all."

Pastor Frank stood, studying him for a moment. Layton felt embarrassed about the way he had tuned in and out of the conversation. "I'll call you—when we get more news about Brianne. Soon, I hope."

Pastor Frank nodded as Layton turned to leave. "God loves you, Layton. And he loves Brianne more than you do."

Sure, Layton thought as he kept walking. *Sure He does.*

Instead of going directly back upstairs, Layton found himself wandering around the hospital gift shop. His eyes were drawn immediately to the stuffed animals on display. He recalled Brianne's massive pile tucked away in her princess tent at home. She loved her furry bear in particular.

He'd given her the white polar bear after a business trip that had taken him away from home for a week. Amy looked tired, and Brianne was fussy. It had been a long week for everyone. In retrospect, he wondered whether he was trying to buy Brianne's forgiveness.

"What are you going to name her?"

"I'm going to name her Paychunts. After you, Daddy."

"Paychunts? What kind of a name is that?"

Brianne explained, "When you're gone, Mommy says I have to have paychunts. Then you'll come home. Now I'll have more paychunts."

"Oh." Layton squirmed in his chair. "You mean *patience*. Like learning to wait."

"That's what I said, Daddy. Come on, Paychunts." Brianne clutched the bear. "Let me show you our room."

Layton couldn't decide if the bear had been a good idea or not. Brianne's response had made him feel uneasy—trapped, in fact. When he'd looked over at Amy, a tinge of resentment began to build. Why did everyone need a piece of him when after a tough week he had so little left to give? He'd settled into his recliner and reached for the paper.

When Layton returned to the surgical waiting room, he carried a stuffed tiger and held a "Get Well" balloon. He looked around the room.

Amy thumbed through a well-worn copy of *Southern Living* magazine. At the visitor's guest table, Beth softly spoke into a phone. Her husband, Craig, sat in a circle of chairs, talking with the few friends who were left. Amy glanced at her watch. "Where have you been?"

"To the gift store, obviously." Layton expected a warmer response. After all, he'd bought Brianne gifts.

"Dr. Holt hasn't been out yet," she said dejectedly. "It's been forty-five minutes, and the patient rep said—"

"Don't worry," Layton interrupted. "She's probably checking on another patient. How do you like the tiger?"

"Cute."

"It's a cat for my Kitten."

"Really cute." Layton caught the tinge of sarcasm in her voice.

Their friends had stopped talking and observed the scene. Layton sat down in the row of chairs directly behind Amy.

"You know," he whispered over his shoulder for her ears only, "we wouldn't be in this space with each other if you hadn't …"

In a nanosecond, Layton wished he could reseal the can of worms he'd just opened. Suddenly, he hoped their friends would stay around indefinitely—maybe forever.

"Mr. and Mrs. Brooks?" Startled by hearing them referred to as though they were still married, Layton jumped to his feet as Dr. Holt moved toward them. Of course, what else would she call them? Amy had chosen to keep his name because of Brianne.

"I removed the tumor, and the cancer doesn't appear to have spread to the surrounding tissue. Of course, we won't know until after the lab results." Dr. Holt appeared confident but cautious.

"Are you sure you got all of it?" Amy queried.

"I believe so. Brianne is in the recovery room. A nurse will come get you when she starts to rouse."

"What then?" Layton interjected.

"She'll be groggy the rest of the day. We'll give her pain medicine through the IV, as she needs it. Let her rest as much as she will."

"Yes, Doctor, and thank you—thank you so much." Amy squeezed her hand, while those gathered around expressed their gratitude as well. While the parents waited for permission to see Brianne, their friends began saying their goodbyes.

"Don't stay away so long next time, Layton. You know where we live."

"Layton, good to see you, buddy. You're looking great."

"I haven't seen Amy relax in a month. You take care of her now, ya hear?"

At that last suggestion, Layton replied, "Sure, I'll see that Amy gets some rest. I'll be around for a few days—at least until her parents can get back to the States." He looked down at Amy, expecting a look of gratitude. Instead, she appeared—well, disappointed. What was that about? He'd done everything she had asked of him.

Brianne slept fitfully in the hours after surgery, and so did Amy. With her small frame draped across the recliner, Amy looked fragile and vulnerable. Layton found himself wanting to pick her up and hold her, much as he would Brianne. Like he did when they would watch television on the couch. Before Brianne. Before the betrayal.

Maybe some of his anger was dissipating. That felt good. Was he finally getting tired of being angry all the time? Brianne had definitely noticed. Yesterday she had broached the subject when Amy left for dinner.

"Daddy, are you still mad at Mommy?"

"Brianne, let's not talk about that right now. Daddy just wants to be with you today. What color marker do you want for that puppy in the picture?"

"Are you coming to our house when I get home?"

"Sure, I'll come stay with you while Mommy goes to work for a few hours each day."

"But I want you to stay all the time." Brianne's eyes filled with tears, and she leaned her little head on his shoulder.

Her reaction stumped Layton. Why did he feel so guilty when it wasn't his fault he didn't live at home anymore? And why hadn't he seen the mysterious Stephen, the heartbroken widower, lurking around the hospital somewhere?

Just then, Amy stirred and opened her eyes halfway, as though trying to place her surroundings. She sat up, stretched, and then looked at Layton with wide eyes.

So I'll ask her, he thought. *Soon. Might as well get it out in the open.*

Since he had taken the late shift, Layton slept in the day after surgery. He managed to grab the last of the complimentary hotel breakfast before running to his car in pouring rain. By the time he arrived at the hospital, morning rounds were over, and he had missed Dr. Holt.

"Good morning, Kitten," he greeted an awake and somewhat aware Brianne.

"Meow," Brianne purred softly. Amy stood at the end of the bed folding a blanket.

"What did Dr. Holt say?"

Amy winked at her daughter. "Dr. Holt said Brianne is the best patient ever and is doing nicely. She let her see her stitches."

"And I can show it to Meme and Papa when they get here! Daddy, do you want to see it?"

Her mother quickly replied, "We'd better leave the bandage in place right now." Turning to Layton, she told him the medical routine for the day. They planned who would have which shifts and discussed other housekeeping details—including some of the bills that had already come in from Brianne's doctor and chemotherapy. By then, Brianne had dozed off, and the two of them were alone together.

"Amy, there's something I've been wondering." Layton cleared his throat and looked intently at the tile floor. "Why hasn't Stephen been hanging around?"

When she didn't answer, he glanced up. Amy looked as though he had pulled a gun on her. Startled? Confused? Hurt? Her expression confused him.

After an interminable silence, she stated, "I haven't seen Stephen since before you filed for divorce." She rose from her chair and headed for the door. "I'll be back after my break."

ை

Amy's announcement left him perplexed. Why hadn't she seen Stephen? The divorce had been finalized months ago. When she returned from her break, ready to assume afternoon duties, Brianne was awake, so they couldn't discuss the awkward issue between them.

"Mommy, hold me," Brianne whimpered. Amy slipped off her sandals and climbed on the bed, putting Brianne's tiny head on her shoulder. She rocked her softly and began to sing a lullaby in her clear soprano voice.

Layton slipped out, and after grabbing a burger at a college hangout on West End, he began wandering around the Vanderbilt campus. The rain had stopped, and a fresh breeze ruffled the leaves. As he walked across the damp grass, he rehearsed his case against Amy out loud to the trees and shrubs.

"You knew I had to travel before Brianne's birth. We talked about how hard it would be for you to handle an infant for most of the week by yourself. Your mom was supposed to help, remember? Then when your dad retired, they volunteered for that overseas missions assignment. Is it my fault they left for Ecuador just before your 'troubles' started?

"Yes, your troubles. I didn't start this. I wasn't the one fooling around. I was in a motel room all by myself at night, trying to earn a decent living so you could stay at home with our child."

Somehow Layton felt better getting it out, even though a few students hurrying to class looked at him strangely. Why couldn't he think of these great comebacks with Amy around?

ை

Layton checked his watch. He still had two hours before he had to be back at the hospital. In the back of his mind, Pastor Frank's question kept burning, penetrating his stubborn denial system. "How are things between you and God?"

The question brought his anger back to the surface. Why did Layton have to answer to God? Didn't God have some answering to do? Pastor Frank couldn't know what it had been like for him these past six months. Who was he to judge Layton?

He walked back toward West End Avenue, past the labyrinth of campus buildings. In the distance, he saw the light poles of the Vanderbilt football stadium. It would be fun to walk past the entrance. He and his dad had spent many Saturdays cheering the home team as they played against teams from the Southeastern Conference.

As he strolled, Layton's mind finally began to grapple with Amy's incredible announcement that Stephen was no longer in the picture. That possibility had never occurred to him. He had assumed the two were together. Maybe making marriage plans.

Gradually, some pieces fell into place. In his recent phone conversations with Brianne, she never mentioned playing with her friend Taylor. Layton certainly hadn't wanted to bring up the subject. He figured Amy had told her not to mention Taylor or Stephen. Although a perceptive and obedient child, would she have been able to talk to her dad in such rambling dialogue about her day and not include chunks of time spent with the father and daughter three doors down?

And unlike that fateful day when his world started reeling, he'd never heard Stephen's voice in the background during phone calls. So, he could only conclude that Amy had ruined their marriage in hopes of gaining another—better—one. Apparently, her plan hadn't worked. Stephen was out of the picture, and Amy was left with medical bills, a sick child, and a broken marriage.

Probably Layton should feel pity for her; instead, he felt sad. Sad and depressed. Still angry. He jogged the last few yards toward the stadium. Remembering great times with his dad didn't make him feel any better.

When Layton entered Brianne's hospital room, he saw Pastor Frank and his wife, Myra, talking quietly with Amy. Brianne played with a handheld electronic game, apparently a gift from the Norwells. She barely looked up as he kissed her cheek.

Amy, standing at the foot of her daughter's bed, looked away. He'd never been very good at figuring out her emotions. Frankly, she'd always been ready to share them, so he didn't have to do much guessing.

Myra rose from a straight-back chair and came toward him with outspread arms. "Oh, I'm so glad to see you, Tony." She held him close. No one had called him Tony since the seventh grade. But then Myra had known him since before he was born.

"It's great to see you too." Layton put both hands on her shoulders and looked at the cropped haircut and slender figure of a once larger woman. He shook off the tears forming behind his eyelids. Myra had been his second mother, and now, he guessed, she was his only mother—at least the only one who knew him.

Myra looked at Brianne, still intently playing the game. "I'm so sorry I wasn't able to be with you and Amy during the surgery. I'm so pleased things turned out well."

Immediately a bolt of guilt tore through him. Never once during his time with Pastor Frank had he even thought of, much less asked about, Myra. Instinctively, he looked at her husband, who was smiling pleasantly. *How embarrassing*, he thought.

Myra turned and draped her arm around the recliner where Pastor

Frank sat. "I had to have a chemo treatment a few days ago, so I just didn't feel up to coming by yesterday."

Layton sat in the chair she had vacated, mostly because his legs gave way. "Myra, I'm not quite following you. Did you say chemo?"

"Yes, Tony. I have breast cancer. I had surgery about two months ago, but the cancer had spread to my lymph nodes. You know me, Tony. I'm fighting hard."

Layton dropped his head in his hands. "I'm so sorry. I-I didn't know."

"That's all right. You've got a lot on your plate right now."

"So, how are you doing?" His question embarrassed him. She'd just answered it. He wasn't comfortable in these situations.

"I've had my ups and downs," she explained. But through it all, God has been my strength. I've grown closer to Him as a result, and it's been a sweet fellowship."

He managed a weak smile in her direction that probably wasn't very convincing. "That's great, Myra."

Layton pondered what she'd said. Myra had grown closer to God. In his own pain, God had grown more distant. Or had he created the distance? He shoved the question to the back of his mind.

ꕥ

Meanwhile, Amy had helped Brianne manage her dinner and then straightened her covers. "Goodnight, sweetie. Mommy will be back later. You get some good sleep now."

"I will, Mommy, because I'm going home tomorrow. I'll show Daddy how I can ride my bike."

Everyone laughed at the child's enthusiasm. Her dad cautioned, "Whoa, Kitten. I think that can wait a few days."

When Brianne fell asleep, Amy and Myra left for a meal that didn't involve cafeteria food. Layton felt relieved that they were gone yet somehow offended that Myra had befriended her. And he was once again in the uncomfortable presence of Pastor Frank.

Layton took a deep breath. "I need to apologize," he began. "I had no idea you were going through this cancer thing too."

"No need to apologize. It affects several of the families in our congregation, so we certainly don't feel alone. Although I have no idea how I would function without my wife of thirty-two years, I can't fathom dealing with cancer in a small child. I admire your courage, Layton."

Courage? Layton had no courage. He was putting one foot in front of the other. "You just do what you have to do," he offered lamely. "Since when did Myra and Amy become friends?"

"As soon as we got news of Brianne's diagnosis. Similar problems tend to bring people together. We really never got to know Amy during your marriage."

"Well, I traveled a lot with my business. Weekends were kind of hectic."

"I know how that goes. They're pretty hectic in my house too." The minister chuckled, and Layton couldn't help grinning also.

Pastor Frank grew serious. "Myra and I have spent quite a bit of time with Amy over the past few weeks." He paused and shuffled uncomfortably. "When you and I were talking during the divorce process, I believe I let you down."

"No way," Layton interjected. "I don't know what I would have done without your support."

He continued, "Amy didn't reach out to us, and since she never really joined the church, I'm embarrassed to say we didn't seek her out. As a result, I didn't have a full perspective on what went on between you two. I'm afraid my counsel to you suffered as a result."

"What are you saying?" Layton's defenses went sky-high.

"I think you and Amy need to talk."

When the women returned and all of them left for their homes, Layton sat alone in the hospital room. He watched his sleeping child and thought about his conversation with Pastor Frank. He knew he wanted to find out more about what happened between Amy and Stephen, but what else did he need to know that would involve Pastor Frank?

His imagination ran the spectrum. If Amy wasn't involved with anyone now, what did that mean for him? For his feelings for her? He thought back to their college days, when loving her was the easiest thing he'd ever done.

He defined love as feeling good when you were with another person, being able to count on them, respecting them. Amy was pretty without being too aware of it. As they drove, she'd let her hair blow in the wind without reaching for a comb. She didn't fuss over her makeup. And she had made him feel good about himself—strong, capable, dependable.

During their marriage, he'd admired the way Amy held down the fort while he traveled, and she was a terrific mother. But Layton knew he'd taken his relationship with Amy for granted, much as he had his relationship with God. They'd sporadically attended church, but Amy felt like an outsider. He hadn't pushed the idea.

Layton tried to dissect the faith he'd grown up with. He thought of it more as faith in a plan than in a person. The plan resembled skull practice before a football game. Work your plan, stay with the basics, don't play into the opposing team's hands, and eventually you'll make a touchdown. Layton thought that advice worked for all of life.

Stay out of trouble, and you'll be okay. Get an education, and you'll always find a job. Eat right. Exercise. Floss. Live God's way. Pray when you get in a tight spot. Don't consciously offend God. If you do, at least say you're sorry. Be nice to people; they'll return the favor. That was the plan.

His relationship with God had seemed a foregone conclusion, not needing close examination. His faith had never been severely tested until his father's death. Now, after the shock of his mother's diagnosis, the divorce, and the divine injustice of Brianne's cancer, the game clock ticked downward.

Obviously, his game plan wasn't working.

Layton and Amy were both on edge, waiting for Dr. Holt to sign the dismissal papers. Earlier, she had come by for a final look at Brianne's incision. Although the lab results weren't back yet, she said she felt early detection had paid off. "I'll be watching Brianne carefully over the next months and years, but I don't expect further treatment at this point."

Such good news should have warranted a gleeful celebration. However, Brianne whined to go home. Tension between Layton and Amy hung like heavy fog in the air. Surely Brianne had picked up on it.

Layton finally loaded Brianne into his back seat around noon. He drove toward the house, feeling the effects of three days of a lumpy mattress, fast food, and erratic sleep. Every nerve in his body stood on end.

He made his way down Hillsboro toward their Green Hills neighborhood. They'd been fortunate to find an older starter home surrounded by trees and lush greenery. Amy's decorating skills had transformed it into a cute brick bungalow with burgundy shutters and terrific curb appeal.

What would it be like for the three of them to be together in a place he once called home? Given the chance, would Amy initiate a conversation—the one suggested by Pastor Frank? Why not leave things as they were? He'd almost resigned himself to the distance between them, and dredging up their past again would surely feel like a walk through a minefield.

Pastor Frank had hinted that there were things Layton didn't know. But did he want to know them? What purpose would it serve? His anger, only partially submerged, resurfaced. What had Amy told the Norwells? Surely, they were too sharp to fall for a pity party.

"Daddy, we're here!" Brianne shouted as he drove past their driveway.

"Right," Layton recovered. "I'm going to back in. That way, you can get out right at the door."

Amy pulled her car up to the curb. She hopped out and quickly unlocked the front door. Layton gathered Brianne's small suitcase and a shopping bag filled with stuffed animals, presents, and cards. As he carried them into the house, Amy picked up her small child and placed her on the makeshift bed she had arranged on the living room couch.

Layton came in holding the flowers and Get Well balloon and closed the door behind him. He sat the flowers on the coffee table.

"We're home," Amy announced with a sigh of relief. "We're home."

Layton offered to go back to the motel, but Amy insisted on preparing chicken salad sandwiches—Brianne's favorite. They finished their meal with fresh fruit from the farmer's market near the capitol building downtown. Amy and Myra must have stopped there during their girls' night out.

Brianne yawned after her last bite. "I want to see my room," she announced. Amy asked Layton to start the coffeemaker while she put Brianne down for a nap. By the time the coffee brewed, he had the table cleared and the dishes put in the dishwasher. He filled two cups and added a teaspoon of sugar to Amy's. He set them across from each other at the table. Resigned to his fate, he waited for Amy to take her seat.

Surely she wouldn't have asked him to make coffee if she hadn't wanted him to stay a while longer. Was this going to be the talk Pastor Frank had suggested? When Amy returned, he asked if she planned to go to the office tomorrow.

"Yes. My desk is stacked high. I really need to. Is it ok? I mean—you will be here with Brianne?"

"Sure. I'll stay until your parents get here. My desk is stacking up too." Layton set his jaw. If Amy really wanted this confrontation, he was ready. Bring it on.

Layton had never really noticed the pattern on the kitchen placemats, but the colors began to take on a darker hue. He looked out the bay window. Clouds were forming overhead. Probably a storm on the way. Seemed fitting, under the circumstances.

Amy had her soft red hair pulled into a chignon, but tiny ringlets had fallen around her face. Her delicate features added to her look of vulnerability. She began to open up about her private pain. "Layton, my relationship with Stephen wasn't what you thought."

"What was it then?" he replied evenly, guessing at her meaning.

"It wasn't physical. Between Stephen and me."

Layton shot her a surprised look. "It sure seemed physical that Friday night when I came home early. I'd driven six hours straight, not even stopping for dinner, to spare us another night apart. And where did I find you? In the arms of another man."

Tears began forming as Amy looked away.

Oh, God, not tears, Layton thought. He fidgeted a minute. "Amy, why put ourselves through all of this again? Really, I don't see—"

"Because you don't see," Amy retorted. She regained her composure and continued. "I felt so lonely. Away from Mom and Dad, away from my college friends, just Brianne and me. I had left a great job as an interior decorator to focus on motherhood. My friends from work were busy. Your church friends never called unless you were home, and then if we did go out, you were with them, not me. I felt I had lost you to work, to golf, to backyard barbecues—even to Brianne.

"My life didn't make sense anymore; things … weren't what I expected. I resented the amount of time you were gone. I felt cut out of your life. Then I found myself befriending Taylor and Stephen."

She paused to take a sip of coffee. Layton sat in a sullen slump. "Stephen was lonely too. He'd lost his wife suddenly in a car accident. He was trying to parent his daughter, work, keep house, and deal with his grief all at the same time. I felt I was helping him by taking care of Taylor after kindergarten. I'd cook dinner for them, and gradually it seemed easier for them to eat their meal here. Stephen hated going into his house at night without Leah there. I'd pop popcorn, and we'd watch a movie until the girls' bedtimes. It became a sort of routine.

"Stephen and I only shared our grief—at how life had turned out. He wanted his wife, and I wanted you. We never wanted a relationship with each other. Taylor and Brianne enjoyed each other so much that it just seemed natural to turn to each other with our pain.

"That night you spoke of—when you came home unexpectedly. The movie had ended on a romantic note. Stephen turned to say something to me, and the next moment, we were kissing. I swear, Layton, he had never kissed me before—before you came in."

Layton had had enough. "I guess you expect me to believe that?"

Amy sighed and took another sip of coffee. "No, not really. But I had to say it. For Brianne's sake. I don't want her to grow up thinking I ..." She trailed off.

"And what about what I think?"

"I know what you think. You've done everything possible to let me know what you think."

Layton wondered again if he should offer to leave, so he did. Amy shook her head. He looked around awkwardly. Should he sit in the recliner that had once been his domain? Somehow, it didn't seem right, so he lowered himself into an armchair where he could only see Amy's profile.

Amy rose from the kitchen table and poured another cup of coffee. She took it into the living room, sat on the couch, slipped off her sandals, and rested her bare feet on the coffee table. She laid the pillow from Brianne's makeshift bed on her lap and held her coffee cup near her chest, as though she needed the warmth.

She began as though there had been no interruption. "I didn't hear from you all that weekend. I called your office phone and must have left a dozen messages. I called everyone we knew, trying not to sound alarmed, trying not to be alarmed. I even called your mom, although I knew she might not remember if you had been there.

"Frankly, I found it easy to lie to Brianne. You were gone so much that she just accepted the fact that you hadn't come home after all. When I couldn't hide my anxiety or my tears, I'd tell her I had a headache. She'd say, 'Mommy, come lie down on the couch.' She'd put one of her doll blankets on me and give me a stuffed animal. 'Mommy, take a nap. I'll watch cartoons.' It broke my heart that she acted like the adult while I felt like a very small child in a scary adult world.

"By Monday, I felt frantic. I checked your schedule on my calendar, called the office, and asked for you. The receptionist said, 'Just a minute,' as though you would answer, but the phone rang and rang.

"I panicked. If you had hurt yourself because of what you'd seen, I—I could never have forgiven myself. Finally, I traced you to the meeting in St. Louis. You said you'd get back to me. By Tuesday, I was very angry about your disappearing act. I didn't hear another word until you called on Thursday to say you'd come by Friday evening to pick up a few of your things and take Brianne to the playground.

"I couldn't face you, Layton. I told Brianne I needed to weed the flower garden in the backyard and asked her to wait in front of the window in the living room. You came and went without looking for me, and then when you brought her home, you tucked Brianne into bed and left. You left so that I had to explain to her in the morning why you weren't here. You didn't even tell her you wouldn't be back!

"I kept repeating to myself, 'This is all my fault!' I turned my anger on me. For a long time, I bought into your opinion of me. I loathed myself. I couldn't believe what I'd done to you—to the man I loved more than I ever thought I could love someone. I let you have the divorce and go on with your life. I thought you deserved someone better. Someone who could be happy with your schedule and who could love you without the resentment that had been building inside me.

"Then I felt Brianne's tumor. I thought God was judging me. I was so scared I would also lose Brianne." Amy began to sob.

Layton got up and grabbed a tissue box off the kitchen counter and handed it to her. *Maybe that's why Amy fell apart in the waiting room when she heard Brianne had made it through the surgery. She must have worried that her own wrongdoing had sealed Brianne's fate.*

Amy reached for another tissue. "Thank you for not leaving at the first sight of tears. I remember how upset you'd get when I cried."

Layton wasn't comfortable with tears. He wasn't comfortable with much of any emotion. Why was that? Maybe being born into a family of boys. Crying could get you into big trouble with the neighborhood guys. But now he needed to be understanding and show some measure of compassion.

"Amy, I don't know why Brianne had to have cancer, but it wasn't your fault. You're a great mother. I've always said that. She's lucky to have you."

Amy seemed startled by his sincerity. Maybe, just maybe, he could learn to listen.

❧

Amy's blue eyes were still damp, but she continued. "Layton, I know I've just told you some things that you didn't know. Perhaps I should have demanded the right to say them at the time. I felt so shattered by my unfaithfulness and so isolated in my grief. I wish I had fought harder for our marriage. I gave up too easily."

Layton's head reeled. He was still trying to figure out why Stephen wasn't sitting in her living room instead of him. "Amy, you're way ahead of me. I don't get it. If Stephen was interested in you and available, and if you were so mad at me—by the way, you could have told me you were so unhappy with our marriage—why didn't things work out between you two?"

Amy pondered the question. Her eyes grew moist again.

"I can't take much credit for why it didn't work out between Stephen and me. I would love to say that I set things right that very night, but the truth is Stephen and Taylor left immediately—right after you pulled out of the driveway.

"Stephen called the next morning to say he had spoken with his parents about moving to Memphis. They could watch Taylor while he built a new life for himself. He put his house on the market the next day, and it sold three weeks later."

Layton couldn't recall seeing a *For Sale* sign in Stephen's yard. But then Stephen's house didn't sit on the way to or from his house. He had probably never looked that direction on purpose.

Amy continued, "I know in my heart I would have chosen you, our marriage. But I can't prove that to you."

"So Stephen made the decision to end it?" Now Layton felt more confident. He had been right about Amy. Both men had left her.

"What could I end? Nothing was happening between us. Stephen was as startled as you and I were by that kiss. He is a good man, a kind man. He didn't want to be a home wrecker. He would never have felt good about himself had he done that to you—to us."

"So why didn't he ever tell me this? Why didn't he face me like a man?"

"Because you disappeared!" Amy showed her frustration. "By the time you were back from your next trip and had moved to your mother's house, his house was under contract, and he had a thousand things to do to get ready to move.

"I'm not making excuses for him. I guess he could have gotten in touch with you somehow, but he probably assumed I had explained everything to you. But you came and went only to get and return Brianne.

"Meanwhile, I was a lot more concerned about losing you than whether or not you got a proper apology from Stephen. When reality settled in—when I realized you were leaving me—I guess I gave up trying to straighten out the mess. My guilt weighed so heavily on me that bearing Stephen's guilt came naturally.

"I know if I asked him, even now, he would be glad to ask your forgiveness. Would that change anything?"

Now Layton needed to ponder a question.

During the awkward silence following Amy's question, they heard Brianne stirring. Amy got up to check on her. Minutes later, Layton recognized the opening song from one of Brianne's favorite videos. He watched as Amy pulled the door to Brianne's room almost shut and walked back into the kitchen. She slowly poured herself another cup of coffee and, looking his direction, motioned to ask if he wanted a refill. He shook his head.

Amy sank into the couch. Feeling the ball was still in his court, Layton asked what seemed a safe question. "So how did you become friends with the Norwells?" Although he had heard part of the story from Pastor Frank, he wanted to hear Amy's version.

She basically relayed the same information but spoke of their relationship with awe and wonder. She beamed as she explained how she and Myra bonded over their mutual struggle with cancer. "Pastor Frank and Myra wouldn't let me stay in the hole I had dug for myself. They believed I was worth salvaging, and gradually, I came to believe that too.

"They showed me such love. Such incredible love. I thought they were just being nice at first because of their relationship with you. But they kept calling or bringing by dinner, and I soon found myself asking for advice about things—like what to say to Brianne about her tumor.

"My mom and dad were in the mountains of Ecuador, completing their missionary assignment. We could rarely get phone service. My dear friend Beth had no clue what to say to me. Myra became a mother figure, one I desperately needed. Gradually, both of them began talking to me about spiritual things, and I began to get it."

"Get what?" Layton asked.
"What life is all about."

❧

Layton had no clue where Amy was heading with her answer. He made a mental note to ask more about the *spiritual things* the Norwells had shared. He quickly catalogued what he knew of Amy's background. She had grown up in a home of nominal churchgoers—the Christmas and Easter variety. No one said prayers around the table or mentioned God in everyday conversation.

Then after Amy and he started dating, the Dyers began to mention their friendship with new neighbors. The Kirklands invited them to musical programs at their church. Over time, they persuaded the Dyers to attend a Bible study in their home. Several months later, both Jan and Phil accepted Christ. Amy laughingly described them as born-again religious nuts.

After their marriage and move back to his hometown of Nashville, they'd attended the church he'd grown up in. Amy had willingly gone with him. He wondered now why he'd never really discussed his faith with her.

He knew Amy hadn't plugged in with his church friends. She'd said being around them felt like trying to break into a clique, one that spoke a different language. Eventually, with his travel schedule, they'd stopped attending regularly. Church attendance fell off his weekly to-do list.

Layton remembered telling her that when Brianne got older, they'd get involved in church again. He wanted Brianne to grow up as he had, with good friends from good homes—the kind of people who went to church.

Still, Layton had considered himself a religious man. Occasionally, in his hotel room, he would read the Gideon Bible on the bedside table and pray—for Amy, Brianne, his mother, and his brother, Kyle; for their safety and health; for the right business decisions.

He seldom spent time reflecting on his sins or praising his Creator. And he didn't give a lot of thought to the rest of creation. Prayer resembled pulling the emergency brake while parked on a steep hill. You might not need the extra precaution, but then again—you might.

The sting of Amy's infidelity had hurt his pride. He'd been blindsided by it and didn't know how to move past it, how to extend grace. Despite his religious upbringing, Layton's predictable God had thrown him a curve ball, and he'd swung and missed.

Now, Layton's own faith hung in the balance. He'd moved away from God, while Amy seemed to be moving closer. None of this made much sense. Layton rearranged his side chair so he could see more of Amy's face. "Tell me more about the spiritual things the Norwells shared with you."

She took a deep breath and returned his gaze. "When you moved out, my parents reacted with kindness about my predicament. I was so preoccupied with self-blame I hardly noticed. Looking back, I should have recognized their unusual reaction.

"I'd spent my life trying to please everyone. I knew very little about mercy—pardon instead of judgment. Your lack of mercy came as no surprise. I was equally merciless with myself."

Ouch! Layton gulped at the truth of her statement. But he nodded, encouraging her to continue.

"Pastor Frank and Myra loved me out of my numbness and denial. They comforted me while I struggled with shame and guilt. They heard my angry cries and dried my tears. And when I finally asked, 'Why?' they told me about Jesus.

"I saw Jesus's love and compassion at work in the Norwells' lives. They showed me God's unconditional love. I began to comprehend the possibility of receiving mercy from Him instead of judgment. Soon, I just melted into the arms of a welcoming heavenly Father. His love washed over me like cleansing rain."

Awed by her descriptive words, Layton wondered if she'd practiced this speech or if a holy presence had simply overcome her. She glowed as she told how God had wooed and won her heart.

"He forgave me for my emotional affair and restored my self-worth. He gave me purpose for my life, and each day became a new adventure in following Him.

"Through the lonely weeks with a child ill from chemotherapy, I felt God beside me, encouraging me to believe in His goodness and ability to care for my child. And when my knees buckled under the weight of my burdens, the Norwells comforted me with the same comfort they had received from their Father."

Layton shifted positions in his chair. Her words made him feel uneasy. God certainly hadn't gone out of His way to comfort him. Wanting to change the subject, he asked, "What do you mean, that now you get what life is all about?"

Amy pursed her lips in that "I'm going to say something important" sort of way. "It took me a long time to sort things out, but with God's help, I think I have."

She turned her head and looked him in the eyes. Layton steeled himself, ready for what he thought was coming. He had never been so wrong.

Layton had always been mesmerized by Amy's sparkling blue eyes. Now he desperately wanted to avoid them. Surely, what she would say next would further indict his character. Did she have some secret meaning to life that he had yet to discover?

She began, "First, I need to take a step back. Please forgive me for what I did to you."

To say that Amy's request shocked him would be an understatement. He truly felt at a loss for words. Never had he imagined that Amy would ask forgiveness, and never had he thought about giving it. Remorse? Sometimes he felt that. Anger? Always. But forgiveness?

Never.

Layton stammered, starting a few sentences but failing to end them. What could he say? He was in no mood to forgive. Out of touch with his own role in the divorce, his feelings revolved around the intense pain he had suffered as a result.

Finally, Amy took him off the hook. "Layton, I hope someday you can forgive me. I know God has. I hope Brianne will when she's old enough to understand what I did to our marriage. Just please, think about what I've said. I know now my relationship with Stephen was inappropriate. I know I set myself up. I put temptation in front of me and fell right into the hole. I have no excuse."

A lump formed in his throat. Her words left him little choice. He finally mustered the courage to say, "I'll think about it."

The awkward silence that followed broke when Brianne called from her bedroom, "Mommy, Daddy, the video stopped. I wanna be with you."

Amy rose to retrieve their child. Layton stood, glad for the interruption but feeling even more awkward about being here. "I—I need to go. Tell Brianne I'll be here early tomorrow morning, so you can go to work."

He slipped out the door and drove to the hotel. Once in his room, he flipped off his shoes and sprawled on the bed. Needing rest but unable to disengage his brain, he eventually gave in to what his heart wanted him to do. He placed a call to the Norwell residence.

Myra answered on the second ring. "Tony, what a nice surprise to hear from you. Did Brianne make it home from the hospital?"

"Yes, yes, she did." Jumbled thoughts rattled his train of thought.

After a pause, Myra asked, "Did you want to speak to Frank? I'm afraid he's not here right now. Have you tried the church office?"

"No. Actually, I wanted to talk to you. I just left Amy's, and—and she told me how you and Pastor Frank had led her to a relationship with Christ. I—I didn't know."

"Oh, it's so wonderful. I can't thank my Savior enough for letting us play a small part in her spiritual journey."

"Sounds to me like you played a big part." He felt her smile on the other end of the line. She'd never take credit. "Myra, I need to talk to you. Do you have a minute?"

"For you, anytime," she replied. "What's going on?"

Always uncomfortable with sharing his feelings, he tried to think of a smooth transition. Giving up, he blurted, "I'm mad about Brianne's cancer. Now I find out that the most saintly woman I know also suffers with this disease. Why would God give you cancer?"

"My dear, God didn't give me cancer," Myra assured him. "My genetic makeup, the environment, my lifestyle—only God knows what gave me cancer. But cancer wasn't God's doing. I've had to come to terms with that.

"Naively, I suppose I expected God's protection from such a frightening ordeal. But each week as I looked over the group of people gathered for chemo, I began to ask, 'Why not me?' None of those people seemed to deserve such misery.

"Gradually, I came to appreciate the reality that suffering is an equal-opportunity employer." Myra chuckled. "It offered me the privilege of the fellowship of Christ's suffering and of His power made perfect in my weakness. That's what St. Paul wanted. I've never felt so close to Jesus nor so loved by Him as I have over the past few months."

Although he vaguely recalled the scriptures Myra referenced, he caught her meaning. Everybody suffers at some point and in some way. For some reason, she felt even stronger as a result.

She continued, "Jesus didn't allow suffering to keep Him out of God's will. Neither will I. Suffering teaches spiritual lessons, and I intend to learn them all."

Layton wasn't much interested in spiritual lessons. He wanted his child and his second mother cured. Overcome with the thought of losing them, he whispered, almost unable to breathe the words, "Myra, what if you die?"

"Then I get to be with Jesus," she replied. "Paul said, 'To die is gain.' I'm saddened to think about not seeing my grandchildren grow to adulthood. I mourn for Frank and the boys. But for me, glory it will be." Myra grinned at her poetry.

"I wish I had that kind of faith," Layton stammered.

"Oh, you can. And I believe you will. I'm praying for you, Tony."

When they ended their call, Layton tried to form a prayer thought, something to get him started in the direction of reconciling his relationship with God. The words stuck in his throat.

He could let Myra go if it came to that. Brianne's life—a different story. He would fight for Brianne's life, even if it meant offering his very soul in exchange.

*

Amy turned off the bedside lamp and crept out of Brianne's room. Her daughter had been fussy all evening. She trudged to her own room, weary to the bone, as her mom would say. Thoughts of her mother lifted her sagging spirit. Amy's parents had finally found a temporary replacement for them in Ecuador and had purchased plane tickets for Nashville. In less than a week, Amy would embrace them.

As she changed into her nightgown, another of her mom's sayings sprang to mind. At the close of their few phone calls across the continents, her mom would always say, "Honey, God's up to something."

At first, Amy wondered what her mother meant by that. But since the divorce and Brianne's diagnosis, she'd found great comfort in those words. She'd given her mom a new nickname. "Mom, you're a beam of hope in my darkness."

So far, hope prevailed—so strong, in fact, that doubt and despair hadn't gained the upper hand. Times of joy and peace shouldn't be based on circumstances, she'd learned, but on the person of God. Surely, He would use Brianne's cancer as a blessing and not a curse.

God had spared Brianne for now. Nothing—not even the conversation with Layton or her irritable child—would take away her joy. She breathed a prayer of thanksgiving.

Layton hurried to his car, aware that Amy wanted to get to her office early. He pulled out of the hotel parking lot and maneuvered his way to Green Hills, which lay just beyond the 440 Loop. He sipped the to-go coffee he'd grabbed on the way out of the lobby.

He knew he'd have a good time playing with Brianne today. That part was easy. The hard part would come when Amy returned from work. He planned to have Brianne down for a nap so he and Amy could continue their talk.

After his conversation with Myra the day before, he'd had way too much time to think. It seemed increasing clear to him that he'd not just jumped to conclusions about Amy's relationship with Stephen. He'd taken a flying leap.

Now she'd asked him for forgiveness. Didn't he owe her an apology? He'd been totally wrapped up in his own reactions and assumptions. He'd given no thought to how Brianne had perceived his actions. Somehow, someway, he needed more pieces to the puzzle. And he intended to fill in the blank spaces today.

༄

Layton knocked before opening Amy's front door. He followed sounds to the kitchen, where he found mother and daughter. Brianne sat on a stool at the kitchen island, scooping pieces of scrambled egg into her mouth. "Please use your fork," Amy admonished.

"You said to hurry, Mommy."

Layton came to his child's rescue. "I'll clean up the mess, Amy. You can leave when you're ready."

Amy gave her daughter a little huff as she darted out of the room. "I didn't mean for you to eat like a pig."

"Oink, oink." Brianne giggled when her mom was out of earshot. Even Layton could feel Amy's tension. She faced a mound of catch-up after being away from work for a few days.

"I know the feeling," he muttered to himself.

"Come on down, Kitten." He lifted his child to the floor and began the cleanup process. "What do you want to do today?"

Brianne puckered her lips. "Mommy said I can't ride my bike."

He stooped down to look her in the eye. "You know what? I agree with her. Let's play Chutes and Ladders instead. I hear you're pretty good at it."

Brianne headed to the hall closet. She reached for the games on the top shelf. "Can I have a little help here?" she grumbled.

Her father recognized a little attitude problem with his Kitten. He refused to play the Disneyland Dad role. His perceptive little girl needed a firm hand. A smattering of guilt thudded against his conscience. He'd left all that to Amy. "Please ask for help the correct way," he insisted.

"Please reach the game for me." Brianne stood with hands folded in front of her, looking at her feet. She wasn't the least bit happy with being disciplined. Her mood changed as soon as they sat in the floor, the game board between them.

During the game, she rattled on about her friends and her playtime with Ryan, Beth's son. "He's so cute, Daddy. I want a brother just like him."

Layton's face reddened. As though that would be simple. Game over, he reached for another one from the closet. Soon Brianne became bored and wanted something more active to do. He couldn't tousle with her due to her stitches. Backyard play wouldn't do either. This visit felt more like his Christmas trip home, when keeping a then three-year-old cooped up in a hotel room felt hopeless.

"I know what. Let's look at your baby book." Brianne loved seeing her baby pictures and often pored over them, repeating the words she'd heard from her parents about the events. The problem with his suggestion soon became apparent. He and Amy were together in almost every frame, looking the part of the happy couple they once were.

He shut the book. "It's almost lunchtime. Let's have a picnic."

"Inside?" Brianne asked.

"Sure. You'll have to use your imagination."

"I'm good at that."

"You can tell me where we are and what we're doing." He began gathering what they'd need for the picnic. Brianne planned it all. Fortunately, Amy had left sandwich fixings that easily fit into his daughter's storyline. After the picnic, they watched one of Brianne's videos that he hadn't seen.

Brianne didn't fight the idea of a nap. Layton read her a story, and she drifted off to sleep. He slipped out of her room. He put away the picnic clutter and loaded the dishwasher. *Amy should be home soon.*

୨୦

When Amy came through the front door, Layton waited for her to put down her purse and hang up her coat. He felt like a child in the principal's office at school, waiting for his punishment. In that situation, Claire Brooks would have defended him to her last breath, but in this case, he knew he'd messed up. After playing the role of wounded lover for so long, how could he turn an about-face and admit to his own role in their breakup? How would Amy react?

He would probably get an earful of recriminations about his lack of faith in her. He'd hear how judgmental he'd acted and how inconsiderate of Brianne and her he'd been in the days following the incident with Stephen.

He'd certainly damaged his witness as a Christ follower. He'd shown his anger at God, his refusal to pray with her, and his lack of pleasure in her own turn toward spiritual things. In short, she must think of him as a hypocrite who'd playacted a churchgoing Christian.

He thought about his neglect of his mother. He hadn't even stopped by to check on her during his days in Nashville.

Layton knew how Amy would react because he'd said all of these things to himself. His self-blame game was in overdrive.

༄

Having put on a pot of coffee when he heard Amy's car in the driveway, he settled with his own cup in the recliner that had once been his home base. No longer pretending that he was a guest in his wife's home, he decided to risk being real. He was in pain, emotional turmoil, and needed the soft comfort of his favorite chair.

When Amy joined him in the living room, bearing her own cup of coffee, he noticed she'd changed into sweats. Apparently, she was ready to be real as well. At least he hoped so. She curled her small body on one end of the couch, facing him.

Layton recounted his day with Brianne. Her naptime was slipping away, so he got right to the point. "I've had some time to think since we talked yesterday. I believe you asked me for forgiveness." He swallowed hard. "I was wrong to assume you were being unfaithful to me. I didn't give you the chance to tell me your side of the story.

"I let you take the blame for our breakup. I wanted to blame you for my hurt feelings. You were my punching bag. I never even thought about how you were left to try to explain my absence to Brianne."

He looked away from her. "I even felt vindicated to hear that a relationship with Stephen hadn't worked out. I've been so selfish. I've hurt you. I've hurt Brianne."

Now he looked her way again. "I'm sorry. I was wrong. You're the one who should forgive me."

Tears coursed down Amy's cheeks. "Only if you forgive me first."

"Deal," he said. "I forgive you."

"Then I forgive you. Actually, I did that a long time ago. I had to. For my own healing. I pray my forgiving you will begin your healing."

They sat lost in thought. Layton broke the silence. "So, tell me about life. What secret have you learned?"

"Myra broke the code." She grinned. "Jesus came to give us abundant life, the best life possible here on earth, to prepare us for the ecstasy of heaven. It pains Him when we don't take advantage of the beauty and wonder of each day. He gives us all we need to carry our burdens: the fruit of the Spirit, His own character, His power to resist temptation. And yet we grumble and mourn over setbacks and difficulties. Myra said to keep looking up, looking beyond to the life to come, while giving Him glory for each new day here on earth."

Layton whispered, "Wow."

Pastor Frank sat at his desk chair, elbows on the armrests, hands in a prayer pose. Layton Brooks would join him in a few minutes. He wondered if Layton and Amy had talked through the events that led to their divorce.

When he'd counseled him following their separation, he had dutifully served as Layton's spiritual adviser. But he'd lacked objectivity. Hadn't he also jumped to a similar conclusion about Amy? He needed to confess his role in the tragedy that had driven the family apart.

He heard his secretary tap lightly on his door. "Come in," he called. She ushered Layton into the book-lined study. The men shared a hearty handshake and sat in facing armchairs. "How's Brianne?" Pastor Frank inquired.

"Brianne's a little annoying," he confessed. "She thinks she's completely healed and wants to perform cartwheels in the living room. We're trying to follow Dr. Holt's instructions, but she's tired of being cooped up inside. When I get back to the house and Amy goes to her office, I'm going to take Brianne for a picnic lunch to Centennial Park. She loves to watch the ducks sail around the pond. But that little trip is a secret."

Pastor Frank crossed his heart. "She won't hear it from me."

"How's Myra?" Layton looked pleased that he'd remembered to ask about her.

The minister gladly updated Layton on his wife, who was now undergoing radiation. He paused. "So what brings you here today?"

Layton took a big breath. "At the hospital, you said Amy and I needed to talk. Well, we have. I'm hoping you can help me make sense of it all."

Layton began by relating his conversations with Amy over the past couple of days.

"I really messed up," Layton concluded. "How could I have been so stubborn and pigheaded? I practically tore my family apart with my own hands, all for the sake of my ego." He placed an elbow on each knee and lowered his head.

Pastor Frank rose from his chair and wrapped his arms around Layton's shoulders. The young man wept as he'd never openly wept in his minister's presence.

As he waited for Layton to regain his composure, Pastor Frank tried to define his own feelings. Mixed with tenderness toward his friend was an uneasiness in his spirit. Was he sad that sin had taken such a terrible toll on Layton and Amy's life? Not altogether. His unease was deeper and much more personal.

Layton blew his nose and squared his shoulders. "Well, that was embarrassing."

"No, son, that was a beautiful sight." Pastor Frank dabbed at his own eyes. "Anytime we get in touch with our feelings, God can bless it."

"I never was much good at that. I've learned a lot about what that cost me too."

Pastor Frank had moved back to his armchair and now rested his elbows on the upholstered arms. "Tell me more," he invited.

Layton thought for a minute before he answered. "I rushed to judgment about Amy and her friend Stephen. My hurt feelings were more important to me than getting at the truth, or even really caring about her feelings.

"When I left after 'the incident,' I don't recall thinking much about what Amy might be going through, or what Brianne was feeling either. And I never really came back home. As a result, I lost my wife and, at least day-to-day, my daughter. How did I get so self-centered?" Layton asked. "Was I always like that?"

Pastor Frank cleared his throat. "Well, you were … how shall I say it?… self-assured. You seemed on top of most every situation you faced. I'd use the term self-confident. That's how I would have described you."

Layton nodded. ""Yeah. I always thought that too. Maybe that's why I wasn't prepared for … for being surprised like that. When Amy and Stephen were, you know … " He trailed off.

"At the time, it seemed a pretty open-and-shut case. Guess that's why I didn't do much exploring for the full story. After all, Amy didn't contest the divorce. All she asked for was custody. Maybe we were both blindsided. I think we've both learned a few lessons through this experience."

Pastor Frank leaned toward the young man. "I believe I learned through this experience also." Layton looked surprised and confused. The minister continued, "I counseled you without getting both sides of the story. Sometimes, that situation is necessary when the other party won't talk to me. That wasn't the case with Amy. Myra and I never reached out to her. We assumed the divorce was a pretty open-and-shut case as well.

"We were as surprised as you to learn the details of what occurred on that fateful night when you came home at just the wrong moment. I need to ask your forgiveness, Layton."

The two men sat in silence for a while. Finally, Layton said, "My first reaction is to tell you that you don't need my forgiveness. Strangely, you're the second person to ask me for it in two days." He brushed a lock of hair away from his forehead.

"Frankly, it's been hard to forgive myself, much less someone else. But as I watched Amy struggle with that very thing—forgiving herself for what she saw as her role in our divorce—I realized I needed to be able to do the same. I not only accepted her forgiveness but also asked her to forgive me.

"So, although I don't understand why it's necessary, I forgive you, Pastor Frank. You've always had my back, and I love you like a father."

Now Pastor Frank's wiped tears from his cheeks. "Wow. Thank you. I needed that burden lifted away. I'm so glad we got to know Amy after the divorce. When Brianne got diagnosed with cancer, we sought her out. Not as your ex-wife. Not to help you two reconcile. Instead, to offer comfort to another family suffering with a cancer diagnosis. The result was a wonderful friendship. How is it between you and Amy now?"

"It's really weird. It's almost like we've traded places."

"What do you mean?"

"Well, she's pretty much told me she wants us to try again—not in so many words. But I can see it in her face when she looks at me—like she wants me to hold her and take the pain away.

"Me, I'm pretty down on myself. It's hard to look Amy in the eyes. I don't know how she could still love me. Now I'm the one who doesn't feel good enough for her."

"You're afraid you might fail her again at some point?"

"Oh, I'm sure of it," Layton quickly replied. "I don't know all my faults, but I've come across quite a few these past three days. I couldn't put Amy through all this again. And the fact is I'm still not exactly certain how we got so far off course. I felt so sure our relationship was solid. How could I have been so wrong?"

"You've both hurt each other, Layton. It's going to take some time to untangle the events and feelings that brought you to this point. Don't jump to solve all that right now."

"It's hard. Everything's all jumbled in my head. I thought I loved Amy. I know I loved Amy. But I guess I didn't show it. I'd shoved all that love to the background so I could get on with my career. Right now, maybe I feel numb. I guess that's better than angry."

"It's way better," his pastor replied.

Layton looked at his watch. "I need to get home. I mean to Amy's. The park trip."

"Certainly." Pastor Frank rose. "Can we talk again, sometime soon? I've got some questions, Layton. I need your help in answering them."

Layton frowned. "I doubt that. But, sure, I'll make an appointment on my way past your secretary. Amy's parents are flying in tomorrow, so I'll stop by before I leave town."

After Layton exited his office, Pastor Frank stood by his window for several minutes. The Brooks family had been exceptionally active church members while their sons were growing up. They came almost every Sunday and often to midweek Bible studies and special events. Doing some quick math in his head, Pastor Frank calculated that Layton had probably gotten about four hours a week of religious instruction—or sixteen per month—or one hundred ninety-two hours a year.

Although at first the figure sounded impressive, it amounted to about a week plus a day out of a year. What could a church hope to accomplish in so little time when it ran up against so many competing factors for a person's time and attention?

Pastor Frank knew that he bore some responsibility for Layton's plight. Layton had grown up in his church. He was a product of his preaching, Myra's teaching, their own sons' mentoring. Somehow Layton had missed the very heart of Christ's message of forgiveness and reconciliation. Why had the leaders and teachers not done a better job of grounding him in his faith? Had he, the minister, failed to model God's unconditional love? How had Layton drifted so far away from God?

He still stood at the window as Layton drove away from the church.

The following day, Layton sat in Pastor Frank's office in the same armchair. Sipping the soft drink he'd been given, Layton relayed the news that his in-laws' flight had been cancelled due to thunderstorms on the East Coast.

On a typical workday, he would have been driving across the George Washington Bridge into Manhattan from his place in New Jersey. In the pouring rain, traffic would have been at a standstill. And Nashvillians thought they had traffic problems.

"The Dyers are actually staying in my condo until they can get a flight out," Layton announced. "My landlady gave them a key after I called. Last I heard, they were waiting to see if the Yankee game would be rained out. If not, they're going to watch it on my TV. The season's just started, and there's already pennant talk."

Pastor Frank laughed. "With the Yankees, there's always pennant talk."

"I'm sort of glad it worked out this way—I mean, that I can help them out. After all, it's kind of my fault they had to come home from their mission post. If I'd still been living here, they wouldn't have had to leave Ecuador."

"Why did you move so far away, Layton?"

He took a sip of his drink. "I didn't want to be around to see Amy and Stephen together. When the transfer to the main office came up, I jumped at it. Again, I guess I thought only about my feelings."

Pastor Frank moistened his lips. "Layton, you remember in the hospital a few days ago, I asked you tell me about your relationship with God?"

Layton looked pained. Pastor Frank had touched a nerve.

"I'm not bringing it up because I want to straighten out your religious beliefs or to get you to make up with God. I'm asking now because I need to know."

Layton shot him a look of surprise.

"I'm your pastor. Certainly, I sense your distance from God. I want you to explain more about why it exists, not so that I can fix it but so I can understand it. Shoot straight with me, Layton. I promise you won't regret it."

Layton tested the waters carefully at first to make sure he could share his honest feelings. Finding Pastor Frank open to what he said, he became bolder. Within a few minutes, he almost shouted to God, "I'm so angry with You. You've taken from me everyone and everything that has meaning in my life. And You call that love?"

When he finished, the men sat quietly. Layton couldn't believe the walls of the church hadn't crumbled around him. How could he have said those things in a sacred place? He still had a certain amount of respect for God's power—the God out there somewhere. He felt sure he was treading on shaky ground.

Finally, Pastor Frank spoke. "Thank you, Layton. Thank you very much."

When the older man didn't say anything else, Layton asked, "How can you thank me? I just told you what's wrong with God."

"I believe He's strong enough to take it."

The following day, Amy and Brianne stood at the bottom of the escalator in the baggage claim area of Nashville International Airport. "I'll see them first," Brianne announced. She pointed to her face. "I have the youngest eyes." Amy indulged her grammar. Would Brianne even recognize her grandparents? She had only been two –and-a half years old when they took off for Ecuador. Sure enough, she spotted the couple first and began screaming, "Meme! Papa!" at the top of her lungs.

Apparently, the flow of pictures back and forth and phone calls had helped keep them fresh in Brianne's mind and heart. Phil and Jan raced to see who could get to their granddaughter first. After hugs and kisses all around, they loaded their bags into Amy's car and headed to a nearby "country-cookin'" restaurant. When the waitress came around, they ordered their southern favorites and sat sipping lemonade.

Eventually, conversation turned to the immediate future. Amy explained that Layton was checking out of the hotel where he had been staying and would be dropping by to say hello to them and goodbye to the girls before heading to Cincinnati for the night.

Brianne began to wail, "I don't want Daddy to go to Cin'nati." No amount of comforting by Amy could stop the tears. Unable to hold back her own, Amy began crying also. The Dyers looked at each other and at the people from nearby tables who were watching the drama.

Meme Jan took Brianne in her arms, while Papa Phil moved around the table to give Amy a bear hug. Instinctively, they clasped hands as Phil led a tender prayer for "this little family God loves so much."

After the "amen," Jan announced, "God's up to something! I'm sure of it."

After lunch and the drive home, Brianne took her grandparents to her room "to introduce you to all of my stuffed animals and dolls." Meanwhile, Amy paced the living room. Layton was apparently running late. She could hear the conversation in Brianne's room. "This is Meow, the tiger, and Paychunts, the bear. Paychunts will bring Daddy back," she said solemnly.

Was Layton really leaving? When would she see him again? They'd made so much progress in at least restoring a working relationship as far as Brianne was concerned. Could there ever be friendship—or possibly more?

When she heard Layton drive up, she met him at the door. Once in the living room, he heard Brianne getting reacquainted with her grandparents. Baseball cap in hand, he stood nervously. "Sit down, please," Amy said as she took her place on the couch. Surprisingly, Layton sat beside her.

"I've just come from Pastor Frank's office. We've been talking lately, and I'm … he wants us to … well, he knows this really good counselor. He thinks that if we … you know, go see her together, maybe we can figure out what went wrong and …" Layton looked at his scuffed tennis shoes.

"Oh, Layton." Amy's soft tone pierced his heart.

"Pastor Frank told me about something called reframing. You look at the frame you've put around a picture—like a bunch of events—and then you look at the other person's frame, and together you try to reframe the picture—the situation—more realistically. The counselor helps you make sense of it. He also wants me to do that with God, to reframe Him. Maybe my frame doesn't fit exactly who He is. Pastor Frank is going to help me with that."

"But how?" Amy's wide blue eyes searched his face.

"I called my office. My boss told me they never actually replaced me here in Nashville—you know, with the economy right now. I can transfer back as soon as I sublease my condo. What I'm trying to say is, if you want me to, I'll move back here."

"To—"

"My mom's place."

"But you never wanted to go over there. You wouldn't even stay there these past few days."

"I know. I've got to work through that too. As a matter of fact, I'm going to see my mom after I leave here. Actually, Myra's meeting me there. She's going to be a lot of help … help coming to grips with the inevitable."

"So, you're still going to be here today, tonight?"

"Looks that way. I'll head on out tomorrow."

"Then, you'll come for dinner?"

Layton looked dumfounded. He stammered, "Sure. I—I want to hear about Ecuador and, of course, be with Brianne as long as possible." His eyes pleaded, "You'll help me manage conversation with your parents?"

Amy nodded.

"I think Brianne has them trapped in her room."

"Let's go rescue them," Amy suggested.

When Brianne saw Layton, her smile evaporated. She began wailing again, sobs racking her little body. Layton swept her into his arms.

"Don't go, Daddy! Don't go."

"Kitten, I've got good news. I'm moving back to Nashville soon." Brianne stopped crying but sniffed several times as she lay against his chest. After a while, she lifted her head. Holding his cheeks between her hands, Brianne looked her dad in the eyes.

"It's true. I'll be home, Kitten."

"Meow," she whispered in his ear. "I love you, Daddy."

Amy's chest swelled with hope. *I love him too.*

Relieved to be on the road to Cincinnati and ahead of Nashville's Friday-morning commute, Layton relished the idea of being alone for the next few hours. He needed time to reflect on the astonishing series of events that had happened since he'd left home twelve days ago.

His thoughts stalled at the definite difference in his relationship with Amy's parents. When he had first met the Dyers during a college break almost ten years ago, he found them a bit stiff and proper. The dinner silverware looked like a maze for someone accustomed to family dinners on TV trays in front of a ball game. Layton's family was noisy and informal. The Dyers were quiet and elegant.

They didn't exactly dress for dinner, but their attire was a far cry from blue jean shorts and a T-shirt. Jan would have her blonde hair pulled up in a bun, with wispy curls around her lovely face. She'd always wear a dress of some kind, while Phil wore a tie, if not a suit coat. His already silvery hair and sculpted features made him an imposing figure.

Layton might have been taller than he was, but he felt intimidated nonetheless. He never could keep his hair slicked back, and nowhere in his closet resided a tie. His attempts at conversation seemed bumbling and trivial. Maybe the withering looks from Amy's father had something to do with his discomfort.

Back then, Amy kept a respectful distance from her parents. Passing pecks on the cheeks with her mom and dad contrasted greatly with Al's affectionate bear hugs and Claire's tender kisses. Layton nodded politely at the talk of art and the theater but missed the friendly jabs and mock fighting that went on in the Brooks household. He made it through those first awkward days at Amy's house without a social faux pas, but a weight lifted as they pulled out of the driveway.

After his future in-laws became Christians, Layton's next visit was a study in contrasts. First, Phil and Jan's relationship with each other was warmer, with a marked increase in their interest in what the other was saying. The word *bonded* came to mind as he considered the change—as if someone had tied two loose ends together.

Second, they seemed more interested in Amy as a person than as a showcased product of their rearing. No mention of a curl out of place, a wrinkled sleeve, or a misspoken word. And no interrupting or finishing her sentences. He felt as if someone had taken a nail file and smoothed Amy's parents into a far more likable and relaxed pair. When during that visit Jan put an arm around Amy's waist, Layton observed that his fiancée looked startled.

And last, Layton became less an object of distrust and more a new friend. The Dyers curiosity about Layton's background—particularly his church background—contrasted sharply with the disinterest they'd shown before. They asked him about Bible stories (some of which he'd long forgotten) and his beliefs on certain doctrines. Mostly, Layton sidestepped their questions and avoided taking personal positions. He didn't want to alienate them right before the wedding. Plus, he had few actual positions to share. Most of his theology was hand-me-down rather than personal.

After the wedding and the move to Nashville, the Dyers were pretty much out of his life. Since he was home mostly on weekends, the retirees would visit during the week. He rarely saw them. Amy was still somewhat repelled by their religious zeal. Of course, Brianne was the light of their lives, and she adored them. Then the divorce broke all of Layton's ties with his in-laws.

Last night, he'd expected a cool reception from them. Surprisingly, they seemed delighted that he would be a part of Amy's and Brianne's lives in coming months. Go figure! Their reaction made no sense.

He'd been glad Ecuador would give them a conversation starter. And what a conversation! He had listened in awe as the Dyers recounted examples of answered prayers. Some sounded like miracles, in his estimation. Yet they both seemed humbled by their experiences. One story particularly caught his attention, mostly because it involved a small child getting needed medical treatment. What if Brianne had been in Ecuador when Amy found that small lump? He shuddered.

Layton couldn't figure out why the Dyers were being so pleasant. He assumed Amy had said nothing good about him since he moved out. This unexpected goodwill made him feel uneasy. Why weren't they angry or at least noncommittal? Several times, Layton caught Jan looking at him with something akin to tenderness. He always glanced away.

Had he stepped into the infamous *Twilight Zone*?

❧

Back at his condo in New Jersey, Layton immediately called Amy's house. No one answered. Amy and her parents were probably out shopping. He looked around his bachelor pad and noted that the cleaning lady had been in. Newspapers were stacked neatly on the table. The only sign he'd been gone was a limp ivy on the windowsill above the sink. If only he could keep the condo looking this good until he got it subleased. He quickly unpacked and piled the dirty clothes in the hamper. Tomorrow he'd do laundry.

His phone rang. When he answered, Amy said, "Hey, Miss Brooks wondered if you were at your condo yet. She'd like to speak to you." Layton could hear Brianne in the background grabbing for the phone.

"Hello, Daddy. Guess where we've been?" Without waiting, she added, "We've been to see Dr. Holt. She said I'm really brave. Soon I get to ride my bike—just for a little."

"Great, Kitten."

"Meow. When are you coming back, Daddy?"

"I just got here, honey. It'll probably take a few weeks. Are you having a good time with Meme and Papa?"

"Yes, they bought me an ice-cream cone. Chocolate, yummy!" He could hear voices in the background. "Papa wants to say something. Love you, bye." Brianne handed off the phone and began the crash-bang of helping her mom get out pots and pans to start dinner. Just like old times. Only better. Much better.

Phil's booming voice overcame the noise factor. "Hello, Layton. So you made it back safely?"

"Yeah, no problems. Sunday I'm going into the office while it's quiet. At least the weatherman says I won't have to deal with driving in the rain."

"You don't want that, for sure," Phil recalled. "Hey, thanks again for loaning us your place. Could we take your television back with us to our mission station?" Layton chuckled at the thought of Phil lugging a set through airports and into the jungle.

Mostly, he felt amazed that they were talking at all.

While Layton stacked high a ham and cheese sandwich, he dialed the Norwell residence. Myra greeted him warmly. "Thanks for letting me know you're home. It must be a mother thing, wanting to know your little birds are safely in their nests," she mused.

Layton laughed, then grew serious. "Myra, thanks so much for going with me to see Mom. I don't think I could have done it without you."

"Oh, I'm so glad we went. And to have found her looking and feeling so well."

"Myra, she thought I was Kyle."

"I know, dear, but that made her happy. Isn't that the most important thing?"

"Yeah, I guess." Layton recalled his self-centered ways. In the past, he hadn't been willing to see his mother because the visits made him feel so miserable. Again, her feelings were secondary.

"I know we talked about my meeting Mom's needs right now, not her meeting mine. She certainly spent her life caring about my happiness. It's the least I can do to care about hers."

"That's right. Doesn't it feel great to be giving back?"

"It was hard to leave her, you know? Myra, how am I going to live in Mom's house? When I think about it, I want to back out. Maybe I should rent a place."

"Tony, you can choose your feelings. You can focus on your losses if you wish. Every knickknack, each picture or piece of furniture, can send you into a tailspin of grief. Sometimes, when I think I may be looking at treasures in my house for one of the last times, I almost despair. But then I remind myself of Paul's amazing cure-all for depression."

"Paul who?"

"Saint Paul. You know, in Philippians 4:11. Paul chose contentment whatever his circumstances. He didn't write that because he had a life of comfort and ease. He wrote the letter from prison, of all places! Paul had learned contentment because he had first learned gratitude. Remember, he started the letter with, 'I give thanks to my God'" (Philippians 1:3).

As she talked, Layton heard the echo of his former Sunday school teacher sharing life lessons from the heart. How Myra had corralled a bunch of junior high boys amazed him. Now he had a mind to listen to her words of wisdom.

"Did you know," Myra continued, "that it's almost impossible to feel anxiety and gratitude at the same time? That's why Paul said in Philippians 4:8 to think about things that are true, honorable, just, pure, lovely, commendable, excellent, or praiseworthy. It's hard to find time to feel sorry for yourself if you're thinking these thoughts."

"So what you're saying is that I should focus on the good times in the past. To be grateful for those years instead of the years ahead … without Dad … or Mom." He felt tears welling up.

"I'm not saying it's easy or natural. That's why you need the Lord. His power, His strength is your refuge."

"Okay, I'll try. But I'll need you and Pastor Frank too. When I have a move-in date, you can be on the front steps of Mom's house with your homemade apple pie."

"And a side dish of ice cream."

"Even better."

Before they hung up, Myra said a prayer for him, and Layton didn't feel offended. Maybe the ice in his heart was melting.

೨೦

Three months later, Layton and Amy sat nervously outside the counselor's office, waiting for their first appointment. Although Leslee Baird came highly recommended, Layton wondered if a woman could understand his side of the story. He already felt defensive, and he hadn't even met her. Dr. Baird was running late—a fatal character flaw in Layton's opinion.

He wasn't looking forward to rehashing the story—their story. It wasn't pretty, and he'd made mistakes. Admitting that to a total stranger wouldn't be easy. He wished Amy had gotten all that out in front of her before he moved back. Amy recalled facts and events. He always left something out or got them out of order.

A few minutes later, a couple emerged from the office and walked stiffly toward the outside door. *Didn't seem to do them much good*, he thought. Minutes passed before Dr. Baird came to get them.

A tall African-American woman, Dr. Baird wore fitted jeans with a white blouse and matching denim blazer. He hadn't expected her to be so attractive. He followed her into the room, Amy at his side. A comfortable brown leather couch with its zebra-striped pillows set off the African theme of her office, complete with framed wildlife prints and native carvings.

"So you've been to Africa?" Layton asked after they were seated.

"Yes, on numerous mission trips," Dr. Baird replied. "I managed to stay over for one safari—the sightseeing kind, of course. Then another time, I climbed Mt. Kilimanjaro. Once was enough!"

Layton thought about the implications of her being a Christian. God had him surrounded on all sides, it seemed. Was he ready to surrender?

When the counselor suggested he share the reason they had come, Layton looked surprised that she hadn't started by asking Amy. Something in her countenance invited trust. Like a prisoner set free, he sang like a magpie, giving an abbreviated review of the events leading to the divorce. Uncharacteristically, Layton was open and honest about his role in the breakup and his fears for the future.

"What's your main goal in coming here?" Dr. Baird asked.

Layton looked at her quizzically. She continued, "Do you hope to get back together as a couple or just get past your negative feelings?"

Amy leaned forward, waiting to hear his answer. Layton studied the bold print of the carpet before answering. "I want us to be a family. A real family."

He gave Amy a loving look. Her tear-stained cheeks made him wonder again why women cry at the strangest times.

Once again, Layton sat in an armchair facing Pastor Frank. Reframing his image of God took longer than he'd expected. The process certainly felt as intense as the sessions with Dr. Baird and Amy. Already, Layton sensed his anger against God fading.

In their first session, Pastor Frank had led him through several passages from the Bible that described God's nature and character. He'd begun with God's self-description in Exodus 34:6, in which God called Himself the compassionate and gracious God, slow to anger, abounding in love and faithfulness, maintaining love to thousands, and forgiving wickedness, rebellion, and sin.

"So, how does this match your portrait of God?" his pastor had asked. Months ago, Layton would have called Him "creator, lawgiver, judge." Although these were true, Layton had discovered a softer side: compassionate, gracious, loving, faithful, and forgiving. One phrase struck Layton as pivotal: slow to anger.

"I wasn't slow to anger with Amy," he'd confessed to his minister. "I jumped to conclusions, protected my own ego, and played judge and jury—all in one fell swoop. I'm glad God doesn't treat me the same way."

Pastor Frank had chuckled. "No, we never want that."

They'd moved on from there, reviewing God's covenant relationship with Israel. God had called out a people as His own to bless the peoples of the world and to proclaim Him as the one true God.

Instead, they turned their backs on Him. They disobeyed His laws and worshipped idols. He asked Layton to read Hosea 11:1, 4, and 9:

> When Israel was a child, I loved him,
> and out of Egypt I called my son. …
> I led them with human cords,
> With ropes of kindness.
> I will not vent the full fury of My anger; …
> For I am God and not man.

Layton remembered enough of his Sunday school lessons to know that God did bring Israel back from captivity. "Pretty amazing," Layton mused. "I never really had to deal with something big to forgive before my dad's death. And Amy … I mean, when I thought Amy had betrayed me. No forgiveness there. God had absolute proof of his children's rebellion, yet He chose to forgive. Incredible, huh?"

Pastor Frank nodded. "Faithful love, even in the face of unfaithfulness."

Finally, after working through to Malachi 2:13–14, Layton reread God's words about a faithful husband.

> And this is another thing you do: you cover the Lord's altar with tears, with weeping and groaning, because He no longer respects your offerings or receives them gladly from your hands. Yet you ask, "For what reason?" Because the Lord has been a witness between you and the wife of your youth. You have acted treacherously against her, though she was your marriage partner and your wife by covenant. Didn't the one God make us with a remnant of His life-breath? And what does the One seek? A godly offspring. So watch yourselves carefully, and do not act treacherously against the wife of your youth.

After reviewing images of God from the Old Testament, Pastor Frank asked Layton to reframe his image of God in his own words. He opened a door of his credenza and pulled out an old picture frame, then handed Layton a piece of paper and a black pen. His young friend laughed. "What am I supposed to do with this?

"Write words that describe God," his pastor explained. "We'll frame them."

Layton reflected on what he'd learned. "God showed mercy when a lesser god would have demanded punishment. And His kindness and compassion were really undeserved. I found a softer side of God that I guess I never knew existed."

He wrote, *Passionate lover … jealous for His people's affections … protector … friend … merciful.* He handed the paper back to the minister. Together they placed the sheet in the picture frame. Pastor Frank handed it to him.

"So go home and think about it. We'll talk more next time."

Two weeks later, they met again. Layton got right to the point.

"God is scary," Layton began, and then stopped abruptly. "I'm sorry, I didn't mean …"

"No, no, go on. You're not the first or only person to find God frightening."

Layton relaxed a bit. "I meant what I said last time … you know, about God being loving and all. But you never know what He's going to do next. You think you have Him figured out, and then … everything goes haywire."

Pastor Frank nodded.

"I guess I'm having trouble with the trust part. Trusting His love. I thought God should protect me, take care of me. Then my dad died, and my mom got sick …" He trailed off.

Pastor Frank leaned forward. "I guess if God guaranteed perfect health and a long life, everyone would want a piece of Him." He paused to let his words sink in. "When sin and death entered God's world, they marred all of creation. We're not going to get out of this alive."

Layton looked down, then spoke softly. "I've been blaming Him. I guess I should be blaming the evil one." He turned his gaze to his wise friend. "I needed someone to blame. I couldn't face my fears, couldn't deal with reality. Somehow I just expected my parents to be around to see Brianne grow up."

"And Al and Claire would have loved that. It's okay to miss them, to have wanted a different outcome."

Layton put his hands on his face as tears gathered. "I didn't turn to God. I turned away from Him. I didn't open myself to let Him love me through it." His shoulders heaved as the burden he'd been carrying seemed to lift a little.

"I doubt you could have made it through these losses without a loving God by your side, even if you didn't sense His presence. He's here for you, Layton. He's always been."

❧

Layton had returned home to think about it. Now, once again, here he sat, looking nervously at his feet, rubbing his hands up and down his legs. He'd refused a soft drink, and now the small talk had quieted. Pastor Frank leaned his arms on his chair and pressed his fingers together.

"I get that God loved my family," Layton began, "and my parents' illnesses weren't a sign that God didn't care about us anymore. Both Mom and Dad lived full lives, serving their church and community, doing their best with their kids.

"But what about Brianne? What if she'd died in surgery? What if her cancer had been inoperable or incurable? What would my opinion of God be then?

"I guess I'm still struggling with why a four-year-old child has cancer to begin with. Where was God when He made that decision? Either Amy or I would have gladly taken her place."

Pastor Frank sat back in his chair. "Ah, the 'why do bad things happen to good people'—or children, in this case—question. If I could answer that, I'd be sitting on my yacht in the Bahamas." He scratched his chin and reached for his Bible. Turning to Isaiah 40, he read aloud verses 13–14.

> Who has directed the Spirit of the Lord, or who gave Him
> His counsel?
> Who did He consult with?
> Who gave Him understanding
> and taught Him the paths of justice?
> Who taught Him knowledge
> and showed Him the way
> of understanding?

Pastor Frank skipped a few verses and read verse 25: "'Who will you compare Me to? or who is My equal?' asks the Holy One."

He gave Layton a tender smile. "It's not that we can't question God. Job did when God took everything of meaning away from him. Do you remember God's response?" He flipped back to Job 38:4: 'Where were you when I established the earth?' After an endless series of questions from God that revealed Job's total lack of perspective, Job ran out of accusations.

"Then Job said to God—words I committed to memory after Myra's diagnosis—'Surely I spoke about things I did not understand, things too wonderful for me to know.' That's from Job 42:3, in case you want to memorize it too."

Pastor Frank took off his glasses and leaned in. "More than a few times I've wanted God to answer my prayers a certain way. Instead, He's pointed me in an unexpected direction or said no. I'm also fighting cancer with Myra. But my battle is with this disease, a part of our diseased world. My battle is not with God."

Layton covered his face with his hands. His shoulders heaved as the weight of his concern for his child overcame him. "I can't lose her, Pastor. I just can't."

The minister let the minutes tick by until Layton regained control. He reached out and laid his hand on his shoulder. "The answer to your dilemma is not to turn away from God. Remember when Jesus asked the disciples if they, too, would go away from Him? Peter answered in John 6:68, "'Lord, who will we go to? You have the words of eternal life.'"

Layton and Amy settled into their usual spots on Dr. Baird's couch. She sat across from them with a grin that spread from ear to ear. Layton found it hard to resist her broad smile, so he smiled back, not sure why. "Okay, Doc. What gives?" he asked playfully.

"I think I'm about to lose two clients." She continued to grin.

"Doesn't sounds like good news," he retorted, "unless you've taken a vow of poverty."

By now, Amy also grinned. She turned toward Layton. "I think she's trying to tell us she's sending us on our way after today's session." She looked back at the counselor. "Am I right?"

Dr. Baird nodded. "That's the plan. Of course, you have to pass the final exam."

"Knew there'd be a hitch," Layton shot back.

Dr. Baird crossed her legs and gave him a somber look. "When we began our sessions, you said your goal was to become a family, a 'real' family. What does that look like to you now?"

Layton felt heat spread up his neckline. He needed to say it well—for Amy, for Brianne. Everything he'd learned from Dr. Baird and Pastor Frank melded into his consciousness. He'd not found it easy to confront the many issues they'd raised.

For one, his mom had been a typical stay-at-home mother of two boys, while his dad brought home the paycheck. She'd married him shortly after high school when he came home from World War II. She never aspired to a career of her own.

Dad's duties revolved around yard work and the Mr. Fix-it tasks that seemed to come easy for him. Unlike his son, his dad didn't travel. His recliner was his throne; his sons, his playmates. Playing ball in the backyard, coaching their church league teams, watching sports in the family den—Dad was their hero. He was also a strict disciplinarian.

But the Brooks family model didn't fit his present family situation. Amy loved being an interior designer. Because she juggled work, child, and home care while he traveled, by the weekend she was ready for some relief. When he spent Saturdays playing golf or barbecuing with longtime friends, Amy felt left out of his life and with nowhere to turn for her own need for R&R.

In counseling, Dr. Baird had challenged them to walk in each other's shoes. They role-played with Layton being Amy and vice versa, telling the other what they needed. Then they brainstormed ways to meet each other's needs. Again, he'd been confronted with his selfishness. But Amy had to admit she hadn't asked for what she needed. She'd assumed way more responsibility for the family than her small shoulders could carry.

Once they'd come to grips with the issues that led to the breakup, Dr. Baird asked them to dream a new and more realistic dream if they were to become a couple again. Layton remembered well their initial discomfort in reframing their possible future. Neither had made any promises to the other, and at times, it seemed awkward and even embarrassing.

They'd worked on a more even distribution of household tasks, with Layton volunteering to take on more of a role in paying bills and keeping up with the family finances. "I can take care of a lot of things from a motel room," he concluded. Together they worked out a budget that included a joint budget of their two incomes that would allow for a yard service and a handyman when things needed fixing.

Amy promised to take golf lessons so she could join him occasionally on the links. And Layton agreed to hiking, nature, and water activities in the beautiful Tennessee mountains, lakes, and state parks. All of the discussions, agreements, and even the concessions revolved around learning to be a couple.

Dr. Baird's analysis on that subject stuck in his mind. She'd said, "Being a couple is not a given, just because you put a ring on each other's fingers. For years, you've been individuals either looking out for yourselves or making assumptions about each other's feelings. Love doesn't just automatically change you into a functioning unit. Joining two complex and self-centered people is hard work. Then, adding a child to the mix … that's why I stay busy."

"And rich," he had added with a teasing smile.

ຯ

"Layton, are you prepared to answer my question?"

He snapped back into the present with a shake of his head. The answer he confidently gave required turning to look into Amy's ocean-blue eyes. "A real family loves each other no matter what. They don't give up on each other. They stay in the game, talk things out, work to find solutions."

He paused. "A real family believes in each other. They work hard to build trust. They put walls of protection around their relationships and don't let the wrong people in. And when necessary, they are slow to anger and quick to forgive.

"They aren't selfish with their time and toys. They build memories and remind each other of God's goodness and love. Mostly, they pray together and establish their home on the foundation of God and the Bible." Layton pursed his lips, wondering if he'd left anything out.

"Amy," Dr. Baird responded, "how about you? What would you add?"

As Layton had done, Amy focused her eyes on her ex-spouse. "Family members have to love themselves, too, in order to love others. They have to believe in their own value and respect themselves enough to do whatever it takes to keep the family moving in the right direction. No one gives up on herself or each other." At this, she nodded to emphasize the point.

Dr. Baird's face glowed her approval. Layton scooted to the middle of the couch and took his ex-wife in his arms.

ຯ

Back in his pastor's office, Layton recounted the experience of being "kicked out of counseling." His minister laughed at his slightly exaggerated description of his and Amy's final visit with Dr. Baird. "I'm delighted to hear your words to each other about being a family again. I'd hoped Dr. Baird would be helpful to both of you. So, now I suppose I'd better kick you out of our time together."

Layton grinned. "I have a feeling I'll be getting a few more kicks from you as I listen to your sermons week after week."

"Oh, that hurt." Pastor Frank grasped his chest as though he'd received a direct blow. "I guess you're ready for your final exam from me, now that you've been booted out of counseling."

Layton rejoiced in the easy camaraderie he felt with the older man. He knew he could come to him in the future with his questions about his faith, without judgment or lectures. He cringed at how he'd misjudged his pastor's heart.

Pastor Frank opened the door of his credenza again and withdrew another battered picture frame. Once again he handed him a sheet of paper, this time with shiny red ink. "We've reviewed the New Testament, looking for passages that describe Jesus. Now it's your turn."

Layton wrote, then read aloud, "Obedient … … the way, the truth, the life … … Lord and Savior … … Sacrificial Lamb of God … … risen king … … judge at the end of time … … worthy of all praise."

Pastor Frank interrupted him. "Who is Jesus to you? Make it personal."

He scratched his chin. "I'm being cerebral again." He looked at the red pen. "I'm thinking you didn't give me this color by accident."

The older man winked. Layton wrote: He died to save me … … He loves me … … He cares for me just as He cares for the flowers and birds … … He takes my worries and fears and replaces them with peace and hope … … I can trust Him even when I don't understand … … He's my friend.

He handed the sheet back to his minister, who read it, framed it, and handed it back.

"Looks like I'm going to have to pass you, young man. You've reframed your image of two of the three persons of the Trinity. Do you need to reframe the Holy Spirit?"

He waved the idea away. "The Spirit has been quite active in my life lately. I think I've got a pretty good handle on what He does."

"You're no doubt thinking of John 16:8–11 and His work in convicting of sin and righteousness. But don't forget that He's also called the

Comforter, the Counselor, and the Spirit of Truth. Jesus promised His Spirit would be with us forever. I count on that every day."

He stood and motioned for Layton to do the same. Looking into his eyes, the minister laid his hands on his dear friend's shoulders. "My blessing for you is to finish the race. Live so as to say, as Paul testified in 2 Timothy 4:7, I have kept the faith."

He drew Layton into his arms. They stood that way for a long time, both with tears in their eyes and a lot of love in their hearts.

Autumn leaves floated from the trees as Layton drove toward Amy's. Friday night was date night. He'd called ahead for reservations at a posh restaurant downtown. Keeping up two households required a tight budget. But this night would be special, worthy of the expense. He'd asked for a table away from the busy Second Avenue entrance.

He pulled into Amy's driveway. Not surprisingly, Brianne sat on the porch, Paychunts the bear in her lap, singing to an imaginary audience. She jumped up and ran toward his car. He hopped out and reached for her. Twirling her around until she begged him to stop, he gave her a big smooch and sat her down. "Hello, Kitten."

"Meow. I missed you, Daddy."

The familiar pang of guilt began its assault.

No, I'm reframing it. He set his jaw, listening to the words of Dr. Baird playing in his mind: *Being missed is not an indictment but a sign of affection. Hear it as such.*

"Daddy, Meme says you're taking Mommy on a special date. Mommy bought a new dress. It's red, like her hair. And she's wearing the pearl necklace you bought her when I was born. Do you want to see her?"

Jan Dyer appeared at the front door, grinning like the cat that ate the canary. "The princess awaits Prince Charming," she teased.

Layton ran his fingers through his short brown hair, suddenly self-conscious about his appearance. Hoping his stand-by blue suit was worthy of the occasion, he moved toward the door, hand in hand with Brianne. He paused to give Jan a hug and kiss, then entered as Amy stood to welcome him.

The dark crimson of the sheath dress draped perfectly around her curves and gave her light complexion a glowing contrast. He thought of the line Amy often used: who says redheads can't wear red? The pearls lay snugly around her neck. She picked up a small purse and walked toward him with the contented look of a woman who knew someone special was admiring her. With a mischievous wink, she announced, "I'm starving!"

Taking the hint that she didn't expect him to stay awhile for Brianne's sake, Layton picked up his daughter, promising her lots of play time on Saturday.

On the way downtown, each recounted their week's activities. Amy described a few of her design projects, realizing most of it would fly over his head. He did the same with clients and sales but offered a few snippets of humor always to be found when dealing with the public. Soon, Amy turned to the issue she dreaded. "Mom and Dad are leaving Tuesday."

Layton understood her sadness. "They've been so good to stay through Brianne's recovery—and ours as well." He grinned at her.

"I know it's time for them to get back to Ecuador. They've only got a few years before their assignments will be up. They're eager to complete what they feel God has called them to do." She paused, lost in thought.

"I've got to make some arrangements for Brianne beyond the few hours she spends in preschool. Or work from home. My boss is open to that for a brief time. But I have so many client meetings, and all the fabrics and samples are at the office. I just don't know what to do."

Then, as if struck by a thunderbolt, Amy sat straight up in her seat. "Beth! Beth had a baby six months ago."

Layton turned to look at her. What did her friend Beth Braxton have to do with this situation? The last time he'd seen Beth was in the hospital waiting room on the day of Brianne's surgery. He cringed at the memory.

"She's home all day with her son. I wonder …"

Layton let the idea simmer. He had no voice—yet—in Amy's decisions about Brianne's care. He trusted her to make good choices. And he was learning to trust God.

He pulled up to the restaurant's valet parking and prepared to turn over his keys. *Lord, help me*, he prayed silently. The Lord would know why he asked. They'd been talking about it a lot.

"Thanks for a lovely dinner." Amy rested against her chair. "I don't think I've eaten this much since Brianne got sick." She got a far-off look in her eyes. "I feel really good about her future."

Layton recognized a golden opportunity. "How do you feel about our future?"

"Ah … really good." She blushed. "It meant a lot to me that you were able to forgive me for my part in our breakup. I know you found it hard. Dr. Baird called it a signal moment."

"I still can't believe you forgave me so easily. I was in the wrong."

"Dr. Baird helped us look at the situation through each other's eyes. Our new frame includes room for mutual regrets. We don't have to paint the frame lily white."

"Thank goodness!" Layton reached into his coat pocket and pulled out something small wrapped in tissue paper. "You mentioned your parents are leaving soon. Today I decided I needed to have a little talk with Phil before they left."

"Yeah?"

"We had lunch together."

"So that's why Dad changed out of his shorts. He said he needed to get a haircut."

"Well, he did, actually. After lunch. Anyway, back to my story. I didn't have that talk the first time. It seemed right this time. I wanted his permission to ask you to marry me."

Amy took a long breath. "What did he say?"

Layton couldn't control the grin that spread across his face. "He said you were a grown woman, perfectly capable of making that decision on your own. Then he threw his arms around me and squeezed all but a flicker of life out of me. While I gasped for air, he prayed one of the most amazing prayers I've ever heard. Amy, why your parents love me is beyond comprehension. But they do. I'm so grateful."

She smiled her knowing smile. "Well, then, I guess you'd better ask me." Layton unwrapped the bit of tissue. Amy opened the small box and gasped. "Your mother's wedding set? It's so beautiful. Oh, honey, I don't know what to say."

"I couldn't leave these rings in her Alzheimer's unit. I put the case on the dresser in my bedroom at home. But it kept staring at me every night when I crawled in bed, saying, 'Use me, use me.' My mom would love that I'm giving it to you."

Amy's tears flowed, but Layton didn't mind them. Progress!

"Knowing you, you've probably still got your original wedding set. That's good. But we need a new symbol of our love. My parents loved each other to the end. I want to promise you a love that will never quit, a faithful love until death do we part. Amy, will you marry me?"

Through her tears, she managed a yes. "I'll be yours forever and ever."

He leaned across the table to kiss her. Neither had noticed the subdued conversation around them. When wild applause broke out, clearly the proposal hadn't gone unnoticed. Amy's face matched the red of her dress. Layton wiped his own tears, too overcome to notice her blush. He put the engagement ring on her finger and the wedding ring back in the case, relishing the day when the matching pieces would once again be united.

❧

On the ride back to Amy's, the couple talked very little. Each wanted to savor the moment, and neither seemed ready to break the mood with wedding plans or living arrangements.

Back at Amy's, everyone was suspiciously in bed, knowing the lovers would appreciate a little privacy. Layton settled on the couch, an arm around his new fiancée. The ringing phone startled them. Amy quickly grabbed the receiver off the end table before it awakened the sleeping household.

"Hello? … Yes, he's right here. Just a moment." She hurriedly handed him the phone. "The nursing unit on your mom's floor."

"Hello. This is Layton Brooks. … Yes. … When? … … Oh, dear God, please … I'll be right there."

"What is it?" Amy reached for his hand.

"They think Mom has had a stroke. An ambulance is on the way. I'm to meet it at Vanderbilt Hospital's emergency room." Without hesitating, Layton led them in prayer.

"I'm going with you," Amy announced. Minutes later, he'd turned the car around, and they were headed back toward downtown.

19

"But Daddy said today is a play day." Brianne could pout with the best of them. Amy had gone to bed late and was in no mood to deal with it. Layton had promised to call her after Claire's doctor made his morning rounds.

Her mom and dad were finishing their breakfast cereal. "Brianne," Meme caught the child's attention. "Papa and I would like to see your zoo before we leave. Would you like to go with us?"

"Yeah!" Brianne jumped down from her chair and wrapped her arms around her grandmother. "I know practically all the animals' names and where they live," she announced proudly.

Amy gave her mom a grateful smile. A half hour later, the trio was out the door. Moments later, the phone rang. She quickly answered.

"Hey, beautiful. I hope you remember what you promised me last night."

"Um … something about spending the rest of my life with you?"

"Bingo! It's sad how our wonderful evening ended. Please thank Phil for coming to the emergency room to get you."

"Sure thing. How's your mom this morning?"

"I've got some bad news. They're moving Mom to a hospice care facility as soon as she's stable and we can make the arrangements. The doctor suggested I call Kyle home."

"Oh, Layton, I'm so sorry."

"The effects of the stroke are irreversible. She may linger several days. We'll make her as comfortable as possible."

His rational side had taken control, but Amy sensed beneath the surface Layton's emotional rollercoaster. He'd never adjusted to his mom's Alzheimer's diagnosis. Her impending death must be tearing him apart.

She explained Brianne's whereabouts and said she'd be right over. But first, she called Myra and Pastor Frank.

ᘏ

Layton paced the baggage claim area of the Nashville International Airport. His eyes darted from the escalator to the conveyer belt where other passengers on Kyle's flight were picking up bags. Where was he?

He saw the Marine Corps uniform before Kyle's face appeared on the escalator. Moving to greet him, Layton extended a hand, then a bear hug. "Welcome home, Sergeant."

"Good to see you, little bro. How long has it been?"

"I guess when we got …" Layton stumbled. He couldn't bring himself to replay their last visit, soon after Claire's diagnosis of Alzheimer's.

Kyle jumped in, "So what's the word on Mom?"

"Things aren't looking good. She's in a coma. She could go anytime now …" His voice trailed off.

Kyle didn't speak, just placed his strong arm around Layton's shoulders as they walked toward the conveyer belt. In the car, Layton recounted the details of the stroke.

"Unfortunately, it happened the night I got engaged."

"Say what?" The news genuinely surprised Kyle. "Who? When?" In other circumstances, Layton would have kept him in suspense, drawing out the story with as many twists and turns as possible. But these were not normal circumstances, and his present mood didn't allow for bantering with his brother.

"Amy and I are remarrying. When is TBD." They reached the hospital by the time he finished the story. Once parked, he took Kyle to the right elevator, punched the floor button, and headed for the coffee shop, while his brother went on to his mom's room.

A few minutes later, he held a hot cup in each hand as he pushed open the door to his mom's room. He stopped suddenly, surprised to see Pastor Frank standing beside her bed. He handed off Kyle's coffee cup and shook hands with his pastor. Glancing at his mother's face, he asked, "The same?"

The minister patted Claire's hand. "Yes. … Kyle and I were just getting reacquainted."

Kyle shifted uncomfortably. Layton noted the body language but asked anyway, "Pastor, if you're going to be around a few minutes, I want to call Amy and let her know Kyle's here. She's planning dinner for us."

Kyle's pained expression spoke volumes. Obviously, he wasn't eager to continue their talk. Still, Layton sat down across the room by the phone. His call seemed more important than Kyle's comfort level.

∽

Pastor Frank turned away from Claire's bed to face Kyle. "I know a lot has been going on in your life." The minister rubbed his chin. "You've been in Vietnam for several years. Now your mother is in a coma with little hope of hearing you say goodbye. Must be a lot to deal with."

Characteristically, Kyle maintained eye contact but said nothing. Undaunted, Pastor Frank continued, "As you process all this, remember how much God loves you and your family. He offers His comfort and His presence." Kyle tilted his head a fraction. The minister considered his options. No use putting off the most important conversation he'd have with the older Brooks son. He'd only be here a few days. So he plunged ahead. "Kyle, how are things between you and God?"

∽

Layton and Kyle sat in the living room of the house where they had grown up. They'd left Amy's house early to finish funeral plans and rehearse memories to share at the service when the time came. Now they rested before the glowing embers of the fireplace. A mild cold front had moved through Nashville, making a fire unnecessary but at least feasible. Somehow the warmth soothed an inner chill.

Layton spoke first. "So, what was going on between you and Pastor

Frank when I finished my call this afternoon? Sorry it took so long, but Amy and I had a lot of things to discuss."

"A little late for an apology now. Pastor Frank and I were having a come to Jesus moment."

"I thought you did that as a kid."

"Apparently, I wasn't convincing."

"So what did you say?"

"As little as possible. Why are you asking? Have you two had the talk recently?

"Well, as a matter of fact, we have." Layton turned his gaze to the fireplace. "My attitude toward God got all messed up with the divorce and Brianne's illness. Actually, it was pretty messed up before then. After Brianne made it through the surgery, Amy and I cleared the air about our breakup. When I moved back to Nashville, we started counseling. Then Pastor Frank offered to help me reframe my image of God."

"Reframe? I didn't know you had Him framed." Kyle chuckled at his joke.

"We all do, whether we know it or not. It's a picture frame we put around Him, keeping Him confined to our mental image we've painted. Often, we formed the image as kids. As adults, it needs serious updating. You might say we've painted Him into a corner. I think I thought of God as more of a life coach than the Supreme Being of the universe."

"Now you've gone all religious on me." Kyle poked at the fire to revive the embers. "Apparently, you haven't been in a war zone recently."

"Maybe my own personal one. Whether inside or out in the world, our wars often shake up our view of God. We think He should be taking care of every situation so we don't have to go through stuff. Really, He's here to go through stuff with us."

"I'll be sure to share that with my unit when I get back."

Layton leaned against the couch. "I had my come to Jesus moment as a kid, just like you did. Somehow I never really got the part about how God and Jesus and the Holy Spirit work together. I was clueless about the power of the Spirit to really change me. I prayed for good things to happen so I could live the good life. I lost my desire to worship God or grow as a Christian. And look what happened."

"So God zapped you?"

"He definitely got my attention, but no, I made my own choices. They didn't work out so well."

"And now?"

"I talk to God a lot. I've even learned to listen a bit." Layton smiled. "I really want God to be the center of my life, not a side issue."

Kyle stretched and yawned. "Well, it's been a long day. I'm hitting the sack."

As his brother walked toward his former bedroom, he sighed, disappointed in the way Kyle seemed to write off his newly found faith. *My brother thinks I'm naive, out of touch with real pain. … But I know what Meme Jan would say. God's up to something. I hope so.*

Layton watched his mother's chest slowly rise and just as slowly fall. She'd survived the trip to the hospice facility and showed no awareness of her new circumstances. The doctor remained convinced that she had days, if not hours, to live. Her nurse sat on the other side of the room.

Last night had been an emotional affair for everyone. Jan and Phil had said their goodbyes. Phil had looked at the teary-eyed group and explained that although the Dyers regretted missing their daughter's upcoming wedding, as well as Claire's potential funeral, they were eager to get back to Ecuador.

Brianne simply looked confused. She'd decided Meme and Papa were permanent parts of the household, and life would be complete when Daddy moved back home. Instead, her grandparents were leaving for "Cudor," and her father still lived apart from them.

Someday, he'd try to explain everything to her. He glanced at his watch. Amy, Brianne, and the Dyers had left for the airport.

Soon Kyle came through the door, carrying a vase of flowers. Layton introduced him to the nurse and took the flowers to the windowsill. Kyle settled on the pullout couch. "Good thing the taxi driver knew where to find this place. And I grew up in Nashville. The city has really grown."

Layton simply nodded. The two brothers sat in silence. Nothing to do but wait. Two days later, Claire slipped into the arms of her Savior.

ᘐ

After the funeral, the family gathered in the seldom-used dining room of Amy's home. Kyle sat at the head of the table, looking very handsome in his dress uniform. Brianne wiggled in her booster seat in the chair between her parents. The Braxtons—Beth and Craig—sat across from them while their baby slept quietly in the carrier at his mom's feet. Pastor Frank and Myra were due any minute. Myra had asked to rest a few minutes following Claire's service, but she'd insisted the others begin their meal.

Church members had provided everything from the drinks to the desserts. Beth would see that all the containers were returned to their owners.

Layton had prepped Brianne for the occasion. She knew her role after her mom put all the food on the table. "Now I'm going to say the blessing," the child announced. "Please join hands. Dear God, thank You for my mommy and daddy, and Mrs. Beth and Mr. Craig, baby Ryan, and Meme and Papa, and Uncle Kyle …"

"And I'm thankful for everyone Brianne named," Amy interrupted with a wink in her friends' direction. "And thank You that Grandmother Claire is spending the day with You in heaven."

Layton's thoughts immediately turned to his mom's funeral. The service had been all he'd hoped for. Pastor Frank had given a moving tribute to both his parents. Myra had felt well enough to add some personal stories and humor from her long friendship with his mom. He could barely recall what Kyle and he had said, despite their careful planning so they wouldn't repeat each other.

Kyle's departure would be extremely tough. Sending him back overseas … … not knowing when he'd have another leave … wondering when and if God would become real to him again. Fortunately, he promised to keep in touch when he returned to his duty station. Later, after the Braxtons took Ryan home, Kyle and he planned to visit their mom's grave.

Amy cleared her throat, and he realized she had said, "Amen." As they started the dishes around, he turned to Kyle. "I didn't realize how much I've missed you." Kyle waved away the compliment. "And the Braxtons have been really wonderful to care for Brianne while Amy is at work and especially these last few days." He stopped, unable to get past the lump in his throat.

The little hostess spoke up. "Daddy, you know Grandmother is in heaven. Don't cry." Then in her most grown-up voice, she asked, "Mother, may I have some turkey?"

As they took their first bites, the phone rang. Amy answered, since it was still her house. Layton could hear her part of the conversation coming from the kitchen. "Certainly, we understand. … … Get some rest, and thank you again for such a wonderful tribute to Claire." She motioned for Layton to join her in the kitchen and handed him the phone.

"Tony, it's Myra. I'm so sorry, but I really don't feel up to joining you for lunch."

"Not a problem," he answered. "Please take care of yourself."

"Just always remember how very much I loved your mother. I guess I'm used to holding in my emotions at funerals as the pastor's wife, just like Frank has to do. I'm finally getting in touch with my own grief. I just can't stop crying."

Layton felt the familiar discomfort over a woman's tears. He didn't know what to say. "I—I almost broke down at the dinner table just now."

"Oh, good. Sorrow shared is divided in half, so the saying goes."

"We'll all get through this together, that's for sure. Thanks for calling." He resumed his place at the table. Amy had already explained that Myra needed to beg off the invitation to join them.

Layton felt a cloud settle over the meal. Would Myra be the next to leave them?

❧

After lunch, Kyle offered to play Chutes and Ladders with Brianne while the ladies cleaned up the kitchen. Layton and Craig sat in the living room, watching a televised football game, volume turned low. During one of the endless commercials, Craig looked over at his friend. "You've changed so much over the past few months."

"A little." Layton grinned.

"I'd like a dose of whatever you've got. We're both busy, but I wonder if you and I could have breakfast some Monday morning before you leave town … somewhere we can talk."

"Sure." They both knew of Pastor Frank's fledgling attempts to start a men's ministry at the church. Those interested had met for a training session the previous Saturday. Mentoring had been one of the areas discussed. Pastor Frank had encouraged the guys to find a mentee. Was Craig asking him to be his mentor?

Layton shot a glance upward as he considered this possibility. *God, You've graced me in so many ways. What an honor to share Your grace with someone else.*

He met Craig's gaze. "I'd like that. In fact, let's plan for next Monday."

❧

The familiar red rake felt good in Layton's hands. The last of the fall leaves had turned beautiful shades of yellow, red, orange, and purple. Slowly, they were trickling to the grass below, revealing much more of the landscape than had been evident during the spring and summer. Brianne was now old enough to help him rake the leaves, although she spent more time scattering the piles as she dove into them.

As he raked, his thoughts turned to the future. Although he continued to grieve his mother's passing, he found himself looking ahead more than behind. Amy and he had decided on a Christmas Eve wedding in the small chapel of their church. Because of her profession, Amy had an eye for details. The wedding had turned into more of a time-consuming affair than Layton anticipated.

He busied himself getting his mom's house ready to be put on the market, all the while continuing to live there. The realtor encouraged him to let the new owners remodel it to their tastes. His job was to ensure that it would pass inspection. Meanwhile, Amy enlisted the help of a professional for the estate sale. She would style the house for showings after the wedding.

Brianne made sure that neither parent worked on their projects without her close supervision. Her dad taught her to hit a nail with a hammer. She and her mom looked through countless wedding magazines. Saying she helped with selections might be a stretch, but both parents wanted her to feel a part of the coming events that would greatly impact her young life.

Now Brianne held open the large trash bag as Layton loaded the various piles of twigs and leaves. She twisted the sack closed as he tied it with a fastener. In a way, it seemed symbolic: cleaning out the old to make way for the new.

The small chapel glowed with holiday decorations and candles. Layton and Amy stood hand in hand under the archway. The bride and groom carried out the Christmas theme in their choice of attire. Layton had replaced his one blue suit with a black one with a red tie and boutonniere. Amy wore a cream-colored linen sheath with an emerald-green jacket. Her red curls had been pulled into a chignon with an emerald pin. She carried a bouquet of red roses, as did the flower girl. Now the smell of rose petals filled the building.

Brianne, standing in front of them, lifted a shiny black patent leather shoe to scratch her itchy lace sock. A titter of laughter sounded from the group of friends who had gathered for the ceremony. Amy gave her daughter that look, and the child stood straight and still. Her strawberry-blonde curls were tied with a ribbon matching her red velvet dress. A cream sash highlighted the calf-length skirt.

Pastor Frank had been asked to keep his remarks short so the families could get home for holiday celebrations or attend the church's Christmas Eve service following the wedding. Layton slipped his mother's ring on Amy's finger, they said their vows, and the minister pronounced them man and wife. Layton leaned down to kiss his bride.

"Whee!" shouted the flower girl. Her rose-filled basket turned upside down as she flung her hands into the air, dropping the last of its contents.

Layton picked her up and laughed as Myra snapped a picture. Guests, who had known them before the divorce, clapped and cheered. Beth and Craig Braxton, the matron of honor and best man, led the way as they maneuvered down the aisle into the foyer and out to the sidewalk. Layton's car waited at the curb to take the reunited family home—together again under the same roof.

Two months later, Amy sat up on her elbows and wiggled her feet in the island sand. "I can't believe we're on our second honeymoon. Sun, surf, and shopping for a whole week."

Lying on his stomach next to her, Layton nodded. Suddenly, he opened one eye and glanced her way. "Who said anything about shopping?"

Ignoring him, Amy talked on. "I'm so glad the Braxtons offered to keep Brianne while we're away. I love how she plays with Ryan."

Layton rolled over, not sure a reply was needed. He felt one of Amy's reminiscing times coming on and prepped himself to appear alert.

"These last few weeks have been so hectic. Can you believe your mom's been gone four months?" She paused as the thought sank in. "Her house sold so quickly. I barely had time to set up before the first showing, and then two weeks later, we had a contract."

"You did a great job with it, honey."

Amy sat upright and looked over at him. "Do you think I did the right thing giving up my job?"

Layton met her gaze. "You love your design work almost as much as you love Brianne and me. I can't see you being happy without it."

"I know. I've wondered about that."

He hadn't planned to tell Amy his surprise until the end of the trip, but he'd never been good at keeping secrets. Layton stood and pulled Amy to her feet. "Let's go back to the hotel. I've got something I want to show you."

Amy followed his lead, gathering their beach towels and prodding for more information as they strolled to their room.

Layton took an envelope out of his carry-on bag and presented it to her. Quizzically, she opened its contents, then gasped. "A check made out to me. And signed by you. Where did you get this kind of money? Did you rob a bank?"

"Yes, and we're on the lam," Layton teased. He pulled her toward the couch. "It's an investment in Amy's Interiors."

"Amy's … what?"

"The new business you're starting out of our home … at least until Brianne's in school. I figure we may eventually have to add on to the house, but for now, you can use the extra bedroom—since I'm sharing yours!" He poked at her playfully.

"But where did the …"

"My share of the sale of my parents' house. Kyle thinks it's a great idea. Of course, now that I'm the chief stockholder, your shop better produce!"

Amy laughed. "I'll do my best. Thank you, honey. I'm overwhelmed." She gave him a big kiss.

"Oh, and Myra thinks the idea is wonderful too. She's already offered to help you shop till you drop. You'll have fabric spilling out into the hallway."

Amy's eyes welled with tears, the kind he could celebrate. So many of his hopes for the future were being fulfilled. Silently, he thanked the Giver of good gifts. He loved helping dreams come true.

❧

Once back in Nashville, remodeling the guest bedroom into Amy's Interiors took over their lives. First, Layton and Craig added shelving to the walls. Then Amy and Beth painted the walls an antique white. Amy bought a mahogany desk and leather chair, followed by two side chairs in a rich emerald-green brocade. Amy wanted a wide sampling of fabric, but she didn't buy much of any one kind. The shelves filled quickly.

Beth presented her friend with a hand-painted *Amy's Interiors* sign, with an arrow pointing customers to the side gate, where they would enter through the mud room. "I'll only show by appointment," she announced. Nonetheless, Craig installed a doorbell at the back entrance.

Once former coworkers and friends had gushed over her displays, clients began to trickle in. Amy arranged a play area for Brianne in a corner of the room. There the child quietly played with her dolls and stuffed animals while Amy worked. Except, of course, when Brianne felt compelled to offer her advice on fabric samples.

❧

The Vietnam War raged, and the marines sent Kyle home on leave. Weeks before, he'd been flown to Germany with a shrapnel injury—his first and only in combat. Sitting up in a German hospital bed with his left leg wrapped in bandages, Kyle watched the war coverage on television. Each segment brought back the war's brutality.

Back in Nashville, Kyle confessed his mixed feelings about the war to Layton: anger and disappointment at not being with his unit; hope that the beautiful Vietnamese people would find some measure of peace; sorrow at leaving behind the MIAs; regret that so far the US hadn't been able to win the war. Kyle wasn't a quitter. Neither were any of the other soldiers in his outfit. Those who'd left had the awful sense of having failed their country—and had found little sympathy for their torturous ordeal back home.

Kyle really had no home to come back to. With his parents deceased and their family home sold, he flew to Nashville to stay with his only sibling while he awaited his next orders. Brianne appeared pleased to have a new guest in the house, even if it meant giving up her bedroom temporarily. She wanted Uncle Kyle to entertain her. But he was in no mood to play.

In fact, his mood seemed to grow darker as the days went by. His return to Nashville turned into an emotional affair. He was often sullen and noncommunicative. Kyle waved away any suggestion that he might need help with his depression.

When he received his orders to report to duty in Brussels at NATO headquarters, he felt relieved. Another duty station in Asia would rekindle painful memories.

Days before his departure, Amy announced that she and Brianne would be gone all afternoon for a play date with Beth and Ryan. Kyle found himself alone with Layton. He was in the living room watching a game show on television. Layton brought him a tall glass of tea and sat in his well-worn recliner.

"Mind if I turn this off for a few minutes?" Layton asked, reaching the console. Kyle waved a disinterested hand.

"Pastor Frank asked if he could come by before you leave," he began. "I put him off until I checked with you. He's missed seeing you in church since you've been home."

Kyle gave him a penetrating look but didn't say anything.

"So, you've still got a beef with God?" Layton sat his tea glass on the end table.

"No, I'm perfectly fine with God doing whatever it is He does with this imperfect world while I go around trying to clean up after Him."

"Kyle, that's not fair."

"Who's trying to be fair? Who played fair with Mike and Leroy and Juan and Kelsey and all the other friends I lost over there?"

"So much pain." Layton bowed his head. "Bro, I'll never know what you've been through. But God didn't cause it. Sin—pride, greed, revenge—these cause wars. God's plan is the Prince of Peace."

Kyle rose from the sofa and faced the front door. He covered his face with his hands to help hide his muffled sobs. He felt a hand on his shoulder. Wasn't he supposed to be the strong one, the one who took care of his younger brother?

Layton whispered, "This may be hard to hear right now. God really loves you. He always has. He always will."

"Amy's Interiors." Amy recognized the voice at the other end of the line. A former client wanted a makeover for her recreation room. Amy made notes at her desk and surveyed the rolls of fabric lining the walls. Her mind was already in overdrive. Then the hammering started again. "I'm sorry, Kate. I'll have to call you back."

Her design business, though crammed into a guest bedroom, had done exceptionally well over the previous five years. The time for separate quarters had long since passed. But now the new office, showroom, bath, and storage room were becoming a reality. Already, workmen were framing the building on land in their now-reduced backyard.

Layton rounded the corner, carrying some architectural drawings under an arm. "Great news," he announced. "I have room for a man cave."

Amy rested her elbows on the shiny mahogany surface. "I'm ready for the unveiling," she announced. He unrolled the architectural drawing.

"See, if we attach Amy's Interiors to the back of our existing house, I've got at least an eleven-by-fourteen-foot space for a television, couch, recliner, maybe a foosball table. Who knows? You'll have an inside walkway connecting Amy's Interiors to the rest of the house."

They talked about added cost, the construction timeline, and where customers would enter her shop. Once she'd had her questions answered, Amy sealed her approval with a kiss atop Layton's bent-over head.

She recalled that the money to open a business out of her house had come from the sale of Layton's childhood home. It only seemed right that he should get a man cave out of the proceeds of the design shop that enabled her to stay home with Brianne.

The energetic fourth grader had the same curiosity and imagination she'd had as a preschooler. Amy glanced at a family picture on her desk taken on a beach at their third honeymoon, this time with Brianne along. In the picture, the child's shoulder-length strawberry curls were tousled by the wind. Layton held tight to her slender frame, while Amy tried to secure her floppy hat.

Brianne may look like me, Amy thought, *but she's definitely her grandmother Meme. She has that same take-charge attitude and strong sense of self that I so admire in my mother.* However, she reminded herself, both females tempered their inner strength with compassion for others and a strong love for God. She found their tender side as compelling as their outgoing personalities.

She turned her attention back to the shop. Getting approval from the city to open an official walk-in business with signage in their yard had been an uphill battle. Fortunately, a national nonprofit out of Washington, DC, had helped win the legal battle on zoning restrictions on behalf of a myriad of other small businesses that operated out of homes in the Nashville area. It had taken years. Amy didn't care to think about how many city council meetings she'd sat through. She turned in her desk chair and did a little wheelie in celebration.

Visions of opening day danced in her mind. Amy's Interiors still provided a way for her to be home when her child got off the school bus. She glanced at her watch. Only an hour before her child arrived home.

Sorting through the job tickets, she placed them in priority, jotted notes, checked inventory, and stacked the tickets in a neat pile on her desk. After returning the call to Kate, she still had time to stir up some sugar cookies, Brianne's favorite.

In the kitchen, she assembled the ingredients, turned on the oven, and began adding the dry items to the bowl when the phone rang. The readout indicated the call originated in Brianne's doctor's office. Her child had been in for her annual cancer checkup a few days before. Anticipating good news, she wiped her fingers on a kitchen towel and picked up the call.

"Hello, Amy." Instead of the nurse, Amy heard Dr. Holt on the line. Her stomach turned somersaults. Always before, the nurse had delivered the results of Brianne's tests. With a mouth so dry she could barely speak, Amy returned the greeting.

Dr. Holt began by talking about how much Brianne had grown and how she'd enjoyed hearing about her school activities. The words swirled in a fuzzy haze. Feeling as though a bomb were about to drop, Amy interrupted. "Dr. Holt, Layton is here. Would you like for both of us to hear your report?"

"Yes," the doctor said. "I'll wait."

Amy found Layton in the backyard and hurried him inside. She placed the phone on speaker. "Go ahead, Dr. Holt."

"Hello, Mr. Brooks. I was about to tell your wife some of the test results from Brianne's recent checkup. In most respects, she's a healthy little girl. I'm concerned, however, about that small lump on her left leg. Brianne's blood work is back. We need to run some more tests. But I want to prepare you for the possibility that her cancer may have returned. If it has, we need to identify the type and, if my suspicions are true, prepare a course of treatment."

Amy let out a low moan and sank into a kitchen chair. Layton stiffened and went into damage control mode. "What do we need to do next?"

"I've set up a lab appointment for tomorrow morning at nine thirty. After that, she'll go for an x-ray and scans. I'll have some preliminary results by the end of the week. Down the way, we'll possibly do a biopsy. For now, I'd like you to tell her simply that I need more information."

Layton cleared his throat. "I will."

The doctor continued, "I hope you know our staff is committed to the best care possible. We all love your daughter and will do everything possible to ensure her continued health."

"We do know that. Thanks for calling." Hanging up, he searched Amy's worried eyes. "She's a fighter. We all are. We'll get through this."

He took his weeping wife into his arms and held her against his body. She had no words and too many questions for a reply. Suddenly, the shop renovations didn't seem important at all.

&

Layton gripped his coffee cup tightly, stared at his white knuckled fingers, and tried to compose himself. Speaking the words would be hard. Hard for him to say and hard for the group of men gathered around him to hear. Especially Craig Braxton, who along with his wife, Beth, had been at the hospital during Brianne's first surgery. Their son, Rynn, was around the age Brianne had been then.

Blinking back tears, Layton looked at the faces locked in on his. These were all men he had mentored during the past five years. Craig had been the first, then William, Jacob, and Daniel. They'd formed a group, simply because no one wanted to end the relationships they'd begun with Layton. The men met monthly in the back room of a diner on West Twenty-Third.

He cleared his throat. "Guys, Brianne's tests came back positive. She has cancer in her left leg below the knee. Dr. Holt and her team are figuring out the right combo of radiation and chemotherapy. She may or may not be a candidate for other experimental treatments. All we know at this point is that the cancer hasn't spread and seems localized. We're grateful for that. But it's the fast-growing kind—good for treatment options but bad for buying time. We're devastated, of course, but hopeful. We know she's in God's hands."

Craig spoke up. "We've known you long enough to know those last words didn't roll loosely off your tongue. You've shared your testimony of how you overcame your own crisis of faith. We've all got a stronger faith as a result of being mentored by you. Your trust in God's providence is evident tonight.

"Make us a list of your prayer needs. I'll keep the list updated, so you'll only have to make one phone call. We're with you all the way, man. Any time you need someone to share your burden, you've got four places to go." The other men nodded.

They made notes as Layton shared particulars, and then each prayed as they voiced the list of concerns. "Thanks, guys." Layton breathed deeply. "You don't know how much this means."

~

Amy had put off calling her mother in Ecuador. Saying the word *cancer* would make it real. She'd much rather be in denial. She finally convinced herself that delaying the call wasn't fair to her parents, who would want to know.

Jan Dyer cried, of course. Phil, her dad, was attending a missionary retreat and wasn't due back until later that evening. "I'll tell him, Amy, and then we'll gather our prayer warriors. They've heard enough about our precious granddaughter to recognize her on the street if they saw her. You let me know when you want me to come."

"Mom, you're always my beam of hope. I love you." Amy hung up, buoyed by her mother's strength. Surely, with all this prayer support, God would spare Brianne.

Eight Months Later

The hospital surgical waiting room looked pretty much as Amy remembered it. Maybe the chairs had been reupholstered—strange that a design specialist wouldn't recall the pattern. Stranger still that she should have this conversation with herself while her nine-year-old daughter was having her left leg amputated below the knee.

At least this time, five years after Brianne's first surgery, Amy sat with her mother on one side and her husband (not her ex-husband) on the other. The same friends were grouped around them, talking quietly. Beth and Craig Braxton were in a corner praying. Thankfully, Pastor Frank and Myra had come as well.

Myra looked frail. Although her cancer had gone into remission, the effects of chemo and radiation had taken a toll. Still, if Amy had to describe her face, she would say peaceful. Myra combined realism and optimism better than anyone she'd ever known. She often quoted Philippians 1:20–21: "Now as always … Christ will be highly honored in my body, whether by life or by death. For to me, living is Christ and dying is gain."

Amy longed to have such peace about the future. Right now, all she could muster was the hope that Brianne would live and thrive, despite her disability.

One night last week, the Norwells had come by with a bouquet of flowers for Brianne from their garden. Amy and Layton had insisted they stay for a visit. After Brianne headed off to bed, they had peppered the couple with all kinds of questions about living by faith. Amy had asked, "What about all those prayers for Brianne's healing prayed by sincere people of faith?"

Pastor Frank had given her a quizzical look. "Does the surgeon believe the amputation will get all the cancer cells presently in Brianne's body?"

"Well, yes," she replied. "We tried the more traditional routes, plus a couple of experimental ones, but her cancer was fast-growing, and we ran out of options. Removing the tumor and the lymph nodes means sacrificing the part of her leg below the knee."

"But do you see what I'm getting at?" Pastor Frank inquired.

Layton replied, "You're saying God is healing her, in His way."

"And, no doubt, for His purposes," the minister concluded.

Later in the week, when Amy's mother arrived from Ecuador, she voiced a similar conclusion. "God has extraordinary plans for Brianne. She can use her disability to share the good news of Christ with others."

Amy stared at her in disbelief. "Mother, what are you saying?"

"Why, He's saving her life for some good purpose. You just wait and see. God's up to something."

Putting the two conversations together helped Amy prepare herself and her daughter for what was happening right now in the surgical unit. Although she could scarcely understand His workings, Amy had asked God someday to show her the fruit of His plan for Brianne, why she'd had to suffer so much. Her mother, ever the sunbeam in her life, offered the gift of hope.

Then her thoughts returned to Myra. Why had Myra—a pastor's wife, a gifted Bible teacher, and a wise counselor—suffered as well?

"Why not me?" Myra had said, when asked the question. "Christ suffered too. He was sinless perfection, yet He endured the suffering and shame of the cross."

Amy had no simple answers to all her questions. Yet Myra's faith was contagious. And she couldn't deny God's love. How could she have gotten through this without Him?

༄

Layton couldn't sit still for another moment. He whispered to Amy, "I've got to take a walk." She nodded her approval. He hoped to walk off some of his anxiety, to be alone for a while, to feel his weakness instead of appearing strong.

He should have known that being alone wouldn't be possible in this crowd of witnesses to the race he was running. First, Craig ambled up beside him, wanting to know if he could get him anything. Layton sent him to the cafeteria for a fresh cup of coffee. Coffee was provided in the waiting room, but Layton knew Craig needed an errand, something helpful to do. Next, Pastor Frank just happened to be going to the men's room. He kept pace beside Layton, letting silence do its work of grace where no words dared intrude. Eventually, he veered off to the men's room, leaving Layton to his own thoughts and prayers.

Finally, his mother-in-law appeared. "I couldn't sit any longer either," she admitted. "I'm so eager for this surgery to be over and for us to get on with the next chapter in this drama."

Layton winced. "What drama?"

"Why, God's up to something in this family," she said with the utmost confidence.

"Like what?" Layton asked.

"I don't know the particulars. But won't it be exciting to find out?" With that, she headed for the water fountain, leaving Layton rubbing his chin.

Layton stopped and pivoted. Repentance required a 180-degree turn. He bowed his head. *I no longer choose to wonder if Brianne will survive the operation, or if she'll learn to walk with her tech-savvy new leg, or if she'll live an absolutely normal life. Her life really is in Your hands. I surrender any thoughts of control.*

A wave of relief washed over him. His faith was growing. He was learning to trust. What would God do in Brianne's life to demonstrate His perfect plan?

❧

The days turned into weeks and then into months. Brianne suffered, as did all those who loved her. Every painful part of her journey was felt twice over by her anguished parents. Now they were in the process of researching the right prosthesis, one that would have to be replaced as her body grew. Meanwhile, Brianne had learned to maneuver quite well on one leg. Mostly, she tumbled, hopped, and crawled. Her balance amazed them as she used every piece of furniture in the house to get around.

Though the couple rarely talked about it, each wondered if the dreaded cancer was finished with their little girl. The thought that she might have to fight it again brought unbearable anxiety. Dr. Holt declined to say the disease wouldn't reoccur, but she expressed confidence that no trace of it had been detected in Brianne's little body.

Now with their child back in school and dealing well with her peers' curiosity, they resumed their construction efforts on Amy's new workspace. Layton set out to put the finishing touches on his man cave, situated between her former office and the rest of the new construction.

One piece of furniture remained to be bought: a trophy cabinet. It had been Layton's idea, of course, since he was the sportsman of the family. Each of the threesome had won awards, ribbons, and trophies of various sizes, and who knew what the future held? So, he lugged in a five-foot-tall cabinet with sliding glass doors and a carved wooden top and positioned it against the back wall of the room between the windows.

Amy dusted the shelves while Layton unpacked the box containing their treasures. He had fishing trophies along with several from church league sports. Amy had won several awards for her designs (including a blue ribbon at the Tennessee State Fair). Brianne had collected several participation trophies and awards for school events and dance recitals in her younger years. Her one gymnastics certificate reminded her father that she'd begun the program shortly before her first cancer diagnosis.

He began filling the case from the bottom up. Together, the items filled a couple of shelves. *Room to grow*, he thought, with satisfaction. Now, if he could only get a buck during the fall hunting season, he knew just where he'd mount the head and horns.

Then the words of Meme Dyer hit home in a way he hadn't perceived before. Months before, as they were saying their goodbyes to them in the Nashville airport, his mother-in-law had again affirmed that God would show them His good purposes in Brianne's illness. She'd concluded, "I do know her artificial leg will be a trophy of God's grace."

Layton looked again at the wooden structure poised against the wall of his man cave. *Hmm … a trophy of God's grace. A trophy case to display God's grace!* Suddenly, the piece of furniture took on a whole new meaning.

ꝯ

Layton had shooed the girls out of the man cave several days ago in order to get ready for, as Brianne put it, show and tell. Behind closed doors, the girls could hear him hammering nails in the walls, no doubt to hang pictures. He'd smuggled in shopping bags and a table lamp, unaware that a little spy watched his every move. Before inviting the ladies in, he'd borrowed the vacuum and dust cloth, window cleaner, and an upholstery brush. He'd asked about curtains that, when pulled, would darken the room for maximum television viewing.

Amy and Brianne listened to the racket and tried to imagine what they'd find when he finished. Amy pouted. "I can't believe your dad didn't let me decorate."

"Oh, Mom, you'd have filled it with flowers and damask silk." Amy gave her daughter a mock frown.

Finally, Layton stood triumphantly in the doorway and invited the duo in. They were most impressed with his taste in furnishings (although Amy found it a bit monochromatic) and admired the items he'd bought on his own. As they inched their way toward the windows, Layton stood conspicuously in front of the trophy case, awaiting the big reveal.

"Ta-dah," he said as he stepped aside. "Now for the most important item in the room."

With dramatic flair and comedic lines he'd rehearsed for days, he showed off each item in the trophy case, beginning with the lower shelves. When he reached the top shelves, he introduced four trophies of grace, each beautifully inscribed.

"The first trophy is for forgiveness, given to my lovely wife, Amy." Layton placed the trophy in her hands and kissed her. "Without your forgiveness, the three of us wouldn't be standing here—together—as a real family."

"Oh, Layton," Amy said softly as tears formed. "I don't know what to say—"

"You've lived it, honey. No words are necessary."

He then took the second trophy and presented it to Brianne. "This trophy is for a big word you don't have in your vocabulary yet; but as the years go by, I hope it will come to mean a lot to you. The word is *endurance*, and it means longsuffering. In other words, Kitten, you keep on keeping on; you never give up. For example, you're wearing a new prosthesis. Often, it hurts or makes a sore. But you keep wearing it. You're determined to master the use of it. Your mother and I are very proud of you."

Brianne looked up at her dad with a big smile. "I'm not really very tough. But I'm glad you think so!" He leaned down so she could kiss his cheek.

By now, tears were flowing, and his female family members had encircled him with hugs. He pulled two tissues from a box on the end table by the couch. "See? I thought of everything."

"Oh, honey, what a perfect addition to our house." Amy blew her nose. "But there are two trophies left."

"Yes, and I look forward to presenting them soon. The third is for *peace*, best exemplified by our dear friend Myra. She's never wavered in her confidence that God's in control and He can be trusted with her future." Amy and Brianne nodded their agreement. "And the fourth goes to my mother-in-law, Meme, who is a beam of *hope*."

"How true!" Amy fingered the one for her mother.

Not to be outdone by her parents, Brianne parroted her Meme's watchword. "God's up to something."

"I trust we'll be adding trophies for many years to come." Layton returned all four to the case and closed the glass doors. The late-afternoon sun shone through the windows, casting a golden beam on the trophies of grace.

Shortly before the day of the grand opening, Amy invited Myra over to see the new Amy's Interiors office, showroom, and warehouse. When Myra arrived, Layton helped her carry in a beautiful houseplant. "I guess this isn't a housewarming gift. Is there such a thing as an office warming gift?"

Amy laughed. "If not, there is now." She positioned the plant in the corner nearest the window. "A perfect finishing touch!" she exclaimed.

"It gave me a chance to shop," Myra replied, "and you know how I love shopping." Then from her shoulder bag she pulled a small, wrapped package. "For Brianne. She can open it when she gets home from school."

"Oh, Myra." Amy gave her a hug. "You are so thoughtful."

"Not really. You know how I miss having my granddaughters close by. Shopping for Brianne fills some of that need. Tell her it's not a special occasion. It's just because she's a special friend." Myra pushed back a gray curl. "Brianne keeps me on my toes. I love that about her."

"What do you mean?" Amy motioned Myra toward a side chair.

"She asks the most interesting questions. Mostly about God. I think she's convinced I've been to heaven and back and know all about Him."

"Well, don't you?" Amy teased.

"I wish. Sunday, after services, Brianne asked me if God had gray hair, like mine. I told her that if He didn't, He would by the time she grew up." The friends laughed. "I doubt she got the joke, but she nodded in agreement."

Myra sat back in the chair. "Just the other day, I thought back to the circumstances that led to our becoming friends. It's so hard now to think about Layton and you as anything but a loving couple. What a loss if you two hadn't gotten back together."

Amy's face flushed. "We don't go there. Some memories aren't worth the trip back to retrieve them. We look forward instead, counting on God to protect us from the forces that are always arrayed against every marriage today. Fortunately, Layton doesn't have to travel anymore—at least not on a regular basis. We're blessed. … So, how long have you and Pastor Frank been married?"

"Forty years. We'd hoped to make it to fifty." Myra looked down at her slender hands folded in her lap.

Amy started to say, "Oh, I'm sure you will," when she stopped midsentence. Her penetrating blue eyes were full of questions.

"Yes, I'm trying to tell you something." Myra looked up and met her gaze. "I found out yesterday that my cancer has returned. I've been in remission so long I thought I was out of danger. I'm trying to sort my feelings. Of course, Frank and I have a lot of decisions to make. You are the first to know. Let us tell the others in our own way and time."

Amy said nothing because she couldn't. Finally, she nodded her head. Her fears for her daughter were simply reinforced by Myra's announcement. Grief overcame her as tears trickled down her cheeks. She knew she cried for all of them.

"Let's not give up, Amy. I want to live. I'll do everything possible to live. But my life has always been in God's hands. It still is." Myra let Amy sob quietly. At last, she stood from her chair. "I came to see your new international headquarters," she teased. "Are you going to show me around, or do I have to take matters into my own hands?"

⁂

After the tour, Amy stopped in front of the door labeled Layton's Man Cave. He'd added a commercial *Keep Out* sign below, which Brianne had attempted to cover with a big X and a hand-lettered *Come on In*.

Myra laughed and knocked loudly. "We know you're in there."

A grinning Layton opened the door. "Why, Myra, what a surprise."

"Oh, sure, like you didn't know I'd be dropping by."

"Actually, I did. In fact, I have a presentation for you." He ushered her in and escorted her to the trophy case. After explaining the origin and purpose of the displays, he opened the door and introduced his trophies for forgiveness and endurance, along with their recipients. Then he took the third trophy and placed it in her hands.

"Myra, your faith in God's plan and purposes has encouraged us at every turn these past few years. Even as you've fought your own battles with cancer, your peace hasn't wavered. You know God loves you, and you love Him. And that's enough."

At this, Myra blinked back tears. "I humbly accept this trophy of peace. I'll let you store it with the others because I like the company I'll be keeping." Amy grasped her hand and led her to the leather couch.

"Layton, Myra has something to share with you. She would like for us to keep her confidence until she lets others know."

Puzzled, Layton sat in his recliner. His face said it all. *Please don't tell me what I'm expecting to hear.*

Layton looked around at the large sanctuary. So many people attended Myra's funeral service that people stood at the back of the church, unable to find a seat. Policemen had helped him find a parking space in the crowded lots of the large facility. Now a long line of cars was positioned to escort the body to the cemetery.

Myra and Frank's sons flanked their father on either side, while other family members filled in the first few rows. Amy and he sat near the front with Brianne between them. Brianne wept openly, but both parents felt completely incapable of crying another tear.

When they had gotten the news that Myra died, Brianne had wanted to know where she'd gone and when she would see her again. They had tried to answer her questions and give her a heads-up about the church and graveside services. But Brianne had been inconsolable. Today she wore the necklace that Myra had left for her three months before on her last visit to their home. The necklace featured two interlocked hearts.

"These are our hearts," Myra had told her later. "Always together, no matter where we are, near or far."

"You made a rhyme." Brianne had chuckled. "I'll love you, too, even if I'm blue." The two friends had high-fived each other for their mutual poetry. For days now, Brianne had repeated the words: "I'll love you, too, even if I'm blue." She said they helped her when she felt sad about Mrs. Myra dying.

"Kitten, you know she's with Jesus," her dad had reminded.

"But she's not with me. I want to go see Jesus too. Can I go, Daddy?" Layton had rocked her to sleep on his lap, the first time he'd done so in years. He felt the weight of her sorrow. Sometimes he wanted to go see Jesus too. For now, they'd have to bear earthly sorrows as they came. He whispered the words of Revelation 21:4: "He will wipe away every tear from their eyes. Death will exist no longer … because the previous things have passed away."

Six Years Later

The Brooks family had decided to have a big celebration for Brianne's sixteenth birthday. She and her dad had practiced dancing so often that she felt she could complete the steps in her sleep. Her prosthesis complicated their routine slightly.

Brianne allowed herself a few tears as she thought about her childhood years before the amputation, dancing with her dad in their living room. "Practicing for your prom," he'd say. "No way a boy is taking you."

She'd giggle and insist he'd be too old and fat to dance then. Now, even with senior prom still two years away, she had to admit the years had been kind to her father. She attributed his trim physique to an active lifestyle. Plus, she had to admit he was kind of cute. Boyishly cute. And definitely fun to have around.

She knew her dad would struggle to lead without causing her to stumble. He was determined not to cause his daughter embarrassment. Accustomed to her mom's lightness on her feet when they danced, her dad worked to gracefully move them around the dance floor. "Relax, Dad," she'd admonish. "You're stiff as a board."

Brianne had taken enough tumbles through the years that one more couldn't possibly hurt. But she didn't want to spoil her dress. It looked so dreamy. She let her mind drift to the magic evening when she'd be the belle of the ball.

ঌ

Two days before her birthday, Meme and Papa Dyer arrived from their home in Miami, Florida. After retiring from their mission work in Ecuador, they now worked with Latinos in their community and church. They were eager to see Brianne walk on her latest prosthesis.

Amy and Brianne met them at the door and showed them to the guest room. Their shorts-clad granddaughter proudly showed off her artificial limb. Papa commented, "I see you're walking as well as ever. We're so proud of you."

Brianne grinned and took a few dance steps with an imaginary partner. "Ready for the big show."

Meme hugged her tightly. "Sweet sixteen. I can't wait." Soon Layton joined them with their suitcases. He lifted the bigger one onto the bed.

Amy twirled around. "I've redecorated the guest suite. How do you like it now that it's no longer my office?" Both her parents complimented the new bedding and draperies.

"It can't compete with my man cave," Layton bragged. "In fact, I'd like to show you something in there."

Amy and Brianne gave each other a knowing look. Amy grabbed a tissue on her way out of the room. After the couple entered the room, Layton led them to the trophy case. "Meme Jan, I've been holding out on you. I have a little something for you. I was just waiting for the right time to reveal it."

"Why, whatever do you mean?" his mother-in-law exclaimed.

He invited the older couple to have a seat on the couch. He traced the origin of the trophy case and how Meme's own words had been the inspiration for the top shelves, which he'd named "Trophies of Grace."

He asked Amy and then Brianne to show their trophies and explain the attributions. Then Amy took out the third trophy and reminded them of Myra's contribution, 'The Gift of Peace.' "But there's a fourth trophy, Meme, and I think it has your name on it. It's labeled 'The Gift of Hope.'"

Amy picked it up and placed it lovingly in her mother's hands. Layton explained. "If you hadn't given all of us the gift of hope, I don't know how we would have made it through the past twelve years. As I've studied the word used in the Bible, hope doesn't refer to an event that might happen but one that will surely happen. Mother, you've never wavered in your belief in God's good plan for Brianne's future."

Jan clutched the gold object as the tears formed. Amy surrendered the tissue just in time. "I'm humbled, of course, and grateful God gave me the gift of hope. I truly believe what I've said. God has been faithful to bring it to pass. And now, I wonder what God's up to next in this remarkable family." She handed the trophy back for safe keeping with the others. Papa Phil held her tightly. The family gathered around as Layton led in prayer, thanking God for their special sunbeam.

❧

The day of the celebration finally arrived. Bright blue ribbons—Layton's requested color—decorated the banquet room of the downtown hotel. "I've absolutely had all the pink a fellow can take," he told the decorating crew in self-pity.

Beth Braxton laughed at him. "You're so henpecked!"

"You got that right." Amy struck a triumphant pose. "It also might have something to do with the fact that blue is Brianne's favorite color."

That evening, Brianne stepped out of her room dressed for the gala. She absolutely glowed in her white linen floor-length dress covered in lace. A sash of periwinkle blue adorned her waist. She'd swept her strawberry-blonde hair into a chignon, tied with a blue ribbon.

Layton whistled at her, twirled her around, and announced, "Now I won't have to pay for a wedding gown. You can use this one."

"Oh, Dad, really!" she moaned. "This isn't shaped anything like my wedding gown. I've drawn a picture of it if you want to see it. It's in my desk drawer."

"I just want to know what it will cost," Layton teased, patting his wallet. "I hope it will still be in style twenty years from now."

Brianne put her hand to her brow in a mock faint. Then the almost prospective bride kissed his cheek. "I'll let you know when my Prince Charming comes along. I'm prepared to wait forever, if necessary."

Layton held her close. "You deserve the best, Kitten."

"Meow."

⁂

Meme and Papa Dyer sat with the family at the round table right off the dance floor. Meme wore a soft pink chiffon dress that exactly matched Papa's lapel carnation. As Layton and Brianne took their places for the first dance, Amy held up two crossed fingers and smiled at her mom. Meme observed the first few steps of the dancing couple. "You know, if we could pluck a few of Layton's gray hairs, I'd say I've seen that couple dance before. Your daughter looks so much like you."

"Oh, Mom, I've never been that pretty. I'm so proud I could burst."

When the music finished, applause erupted from the attendees, who knew Brianne's story. They'd prayed thousands of prayers for her health over the years; they loved the bubbly, outgoing teen she'd become. Layton turned Brianne over to her date and invited Amy to join him on the dance floor. Other couples rose from their tables to dance the night away.

Meme felt a tap on her shoulder. Twelve-year-old Ryan Braxton stood before her. "May I have this dance?" he asked politely, bowing slightly. She pinched his cheek and chuckled as she rose slowly from her chair.

"Hey, wait a minute," Papa groused. "You're cutting in on me!"

"Sorry," Ryan said with an impish grin. "You gotta be quick if you're gonna get the prettiest girl." The two took off, arm in arm, leaving Papa wide-mouthed, alone at the table.

⁂

Back home, Amy took off her crimson shoes and rubbed her toes. "In exactly three more seconds, my feet were going to turn to mush."

Layton flopped down beside her on the couch. "I'm exhausted too." He slipped his arms around Amy's tiny waist.

"I'm glad my parents decided to call a taxi a couple of hours ago.

They'd never have lasted through the cleanup. So much wrapping paper! And I told everyone not to bring gifts."

Layton drew her closer. They sat in silence for several minutes. "Did I tell you how stunning you look in that red gown?" He nibbled her ear.

"You did, several times. But do you remember the significance of my choosing this color for tonight?"

"Oh please. You know I'm not good at this." He sat up a little straighter. "Give me a hint."

"Lovely dinner, expensive restaurant, you wore your only navy blue suit. I had my hair piled up on my head. Something about happy ever afters—"

"Our engagement! You wore that sexy crimson red sheath dress that made me lose all my composure and promise all kinds of impossible things."

"Only with God, they were all possible." She kissed his cheek.

He moved his lips toward hers just as car lights appeared in the front window. A sputtering engine cut off, and noise from the front porch announced Brianne's arrival.

With accustomed flair, their precious daughter stood in the doorway, striking a pose in her regal apparel. Behind her, a nervous young man fiddled with his car keys.

"I'm home. Right on curfew."

"We're all home, Kitten. Come on in."

Layton sat on the couch in his man cave. He draped his arm over the back cushion as he watched his father-in-law on the other end of the couch struggle with a Rubik's cube.

"They didn't have these gadgets in the mountains of Ecuador," he groused. "Years ago, I could have probably figured it out, but I'm afraid my puzzle-solving skills have skipped a beat over time."

Layton gave a mischievous grin. "Actually, there's only one solution, and very few people in the world have found it. The originator even took a month to do it."

Papa Phil set the cube on the coffee table. "Well, then, why are you making me waste my time with the blasted contraption?"

"You picked it up," he retorted playfully. "Don't blame me."

The older man scolded, "You might have warned me it's addictive."

Layton laughed and picked up his coffee mug sitting near where the cube landed. He sipped the drink, reflecting on a day well spent. Then he broke the silence. "I'm so glad you and Meme got to come for Brianne's high school graduation. It wouldn't have been the same without you. It meant the world to her."

Phil's mouth curved into a self-satisfied smile. "I'll admit we found it a lot easier to fly from Miami to Nashville than from Ecuador to Nashville. But we wouldn't have missed it."

Layton nodded. "I felt so proud of her marching across the stage. I don't think the audience could tell she walked on a prosthetic leg. Do you?"

He paused and then answered, "Frankly, I hope some of them did. I'd like to think watching her take those confident steps made them reconsider a false image of amputees."

"You're right," Layton replied. "She'd never apologize for having limitations. Brianne long ago accepted her disability." His eyes grew misty. "I'm very proud of her."

"As well you should be," Papa exclaimed. "I can't wait to see what prosthetics scientists will innovate in the years to come. But for now, Brianne is quite content with how she walks."

"But still …"

When Layton didn't continue, Papa stepped in to finish the thought. "I think I'm detecting a note of parental guilt."

"Guilt? Why would I feel guilty? The cancer wasn't my fault."

Phil acknowledged his answer but offered no rebuttal.

Layton ran his fingers through his short brown hair. "I think I know what you're implying. Maybe I feel I should have been able to protect my daughter, make things right—whole—but I couldn't. We men try to fix things." He looked to the older man for confirmation. "Maybe I still wish I could fix … fix her leg." He looked down.

Phil scooted closer to where Layton sat and laid his hand on his shoulder. He offered comfort and acceptance with a squeeze of his hand. Phil spoke softly. "Layton, Brianne is a unique masterpiece. One of a kind. Healthy, complete. She needs nothing added to make her whole."

A tear made its lonely way down Layton's cheek. He quickly brushed it away. He stood and ambled to his trophy case. Taking Brianne's trophy from the case, he ran a finger across the surface and read the inscription: *Endurance.*

To himself mostly, he muttered, "How could I possibly want to take away all that Brianne's miracle has taught each of us … … how we've grown in our faith, our love for each other and our Lord, how His mercy has sustained us every day. God has used Brianne's missing limb as a trophy of His grace. How wrong I've been to wish things could have been different for her—and for us."

While the men talked, Meme watched her daughter peel potatoes for the evening meal. "I think this is the first time we've had a minute to ourselves," she observed.

Amy wiped her brow with the back of her hand. "I much prefer looking at you in person as we talk. Telephones are great, but they'll never replace being together. … Mom, you just get lovelier each time I see you. I think it's that eternal glow you have about you."

"My dear, you have me confused with Moses." She smiled as she recalled, "His face shown with the brightness of God's presence on the mountain. If that's what you see in me, I'm honored." Meme sat down on a stool at the kitchen island. "So tell me about Amy's Interiors. How's business?"

"To tell the truth, I've been so busy with Brianne's senior year of high school that I'm afraid I've neglected it a bit."

"That's all right, sweetheart. You'll soon be able to pick back up again. From all I've heard, it's been an exciting last few months."

"Frankly, I'm exhausted. I wish I had Brianne's energy."

"Isn't she training for a half marathon this summer?"

"Yes. Her second. She's up at five o'clock most mornings, running at the Hillsboro High School track. Fortunately, now she can drive herself there."

"The car you and Layton gave her for graduation is a beauty."

"Thanks. She only asked for one recently. With her starting college in the fall, she'll need a car." Amy paused her peeling. "I must admit I don't like the idea of her driving alone in the Nashville traffic."

Meme grinned. "Are we being a bit overprotective?"

Amy straightened her shoulders. "Brianne is a very careful driver. I worry about the other guy."

"Just like all of us parents did. If I remember correctly, your daughter also water skis and rides a bike and—"

"Somersaults through the house. I know. I just wish she wasn't so obsessed with doing everything other kids can do. …" Amy lowered her eyes. Rarely did she mention Brianne's disability. "It's one thing to be goal oriented. It's quite another to be driven. Talk about a type-A personality."

Meme thought about her response. "Could it be that Brianne just wants to make the most of every minute of every day?"

"You mean because she almost lost ..." Amy couldn't finish the sentence.

Meme left the sentence unfinished. "Brianne relishes each new day. She's fortunate not to take life for granted. In Ecuador, parents often lose one or more children. They have an appreciation for daily wonders that I'm afraid we Americans take for granted. The simple things of life—watching a sunset, planting seeds, visiting around a campfire—delight them. And they smile readily. I'm glad Brianne is like that."

Amy plopped the potatoes into the boiling water in the pan on the stove. She wiped her hands and sat down on a stool beside her mother. "She is a happy child. Still, I can't help but worry about her."

"Oh, yes you can." Meme pursed her lips. "Every day is gift. Thank God for each of them. But as Jesus reminded us in His Sermon on the Mount, worry adds no value to our lives."

Amy nodded. She reached over and kissed her mother's cheek. "I needed that reminder."

❧

Brianne bounded through the front door just as her mom put the dinner dishes on the table. "Great timing," her mom observed. "Did you have a good time at the graduation party?"

"Great fun. But I'm glad to be back home." She sat down beside Meme at the table. "I want to spend tonight with my grandparents." She reached for Papa's hand at the end of the table. "What did I miss this afternoon?"

Meme and Papa gave each other a knowing look.

Amy placed her napkin in her lap. "Just a reminder that God's in control, and He always knows exactly what He's doing." She turned to her husband. "Honey, would you say the blessing?"

❧

That evening, Brianne entered the guest bedroom to watch Meme pack for the trip back to Miami. She plopped down on the bed and put her elbows on a sham pillow. "I wish you weren't leaving so soon," she lamented, "especially since you're now retired. What's the hurry?"

Meme looked up from folding a sweater she hadn't needed at the outdoor graduation ceremony. "Being retired doesn't mean we have no responsibilities," she answered. "We have committed to teach a Bible class at our church, for one. There's the food pantry to stock, and we look in on an elderly neighbor whose children live far away."

"I know." Brianne sighed. "But why couldn't you have retired in Nashville?"

"Perhaps someday we will." Her grandmother winked. "But Miami is the place the Lord led us to for now." She picked up another article to fold. "Our Spanish fluency is quite helpful there."

Tempted to pout, Brianne sighed with resignation. When the Dyers retired and left Ecuador for Florida, Meme and Brianne had grown closer than either had ever imagined possible. Her mom said they were two peas in a pod. Brianne just knew she loved her grandmother's optimism and confidence in God's good purposes.

Brianne sat in silence, mulling over her next request. "Meme, would you tell me my family's story again? The story of when Mom began to call you her beam of hope?"

Throughout her childhood and youth, she'd asked her grandmother Meme to recount the story of how her parents had gotten back together after their painful divorce. Her mom and dad had long ago moved on from the subject and didn't relish recalling the events. But Meme knew the story was worth sharing.

During one recent retelling of her parents' story, Brianne had asked her, "So why were you so nice to Dad when he came back to town for my surgery? He had divorced my mom."

Meme smiled. "We were once like your dad: stranded in the ditch of unbelief, afraid to trust a loving God with all of life. Despite our sins—past, present, and future—God still loved us. And He loved your dad, too, not for what he had done or would do but simply because he was His child. How could we not love him? Your dad was a lost sheep, and we knew the Shepherd."

"That's beautiful," Brianne had replied. "But I still don't understand why the divorce had to happen at all."

"You will probably always wonder why your dad came home from a business trip at just the wrong moment, or why you had to have cancer, or why that's the route God chose to restore your parents' marriage.

"Or why the cancer came back, costing you part of a leg in the process. God will never explain Himself to our satisfaction. Instead of asking God why, ask Him what—what He intends for you to learn through the experience—and what your story might mean to someone else."

What would her story mean to someone else? She pulled herself upright and put the sham pillow back in place. "You still haven't told the part about your being a beam of hope."

Meme cleared her throat, the way she always did when she was commended. "Now you're going to embarrass me." Meme patted her arm. "Of course, I'm grateful that my sweet daughter found comfort in my optimism. You were facing surgery, and she had almost lost faith in God's goodness. When Layton presented me the trophy for hope, I was speechless."

Meme sat down beside her granddaughter on the edge of the bed. "I'm not a cockeyed optimist. I know bad things happen to good people. I've seen raw poverty, lack of medical care, death, landslides, and crop failures. Life is hard.

"But I believe even more in God's promises. He's faithful to fulfill them. He promised that nothing can separate us from His love. When we keep an eternal perspective, we can live in assurance that all things work together for the good of those who are called according to His purpose. That's Romans 8:28.

"All things aren't good, sweetheart. God brings good things from them when we're committed to His lordship. Christ is called the Redeemer because He's busy trading the bad for the good. Sometimes His work seems to go awfully slow." She tapped the tip of Brianne's upturned nose. "I trust Him to finish the work He's begun in my life and yours."

Layton crunched on a slice of bacon and waited for his mouth to clear before sharing his newly discovered insight with Craig Braxton. For years, he and Craig had been meeting on Mondays for an early breakfast at a local diner.

The routine had begun back in the day when their pastor had encouraged the men of the church to team up in mentor-mentee relationships. Craig had asked Layton to be his mentor, although he protested that he was unworthy of the title. Craig said he'd noticed the profound changes in Layton's life once he'd learned to reframe his image of God and his relationship with Amy. Since Craig's wife, Beth, was Amy's best friend, the change in the Brooks' marriage relationship had been evident to both Braxtons.

Both men had since moved on to begin other mentoring relationships, but they continued meet weekly to hold each other accountable in a discipleship venture of scripture memory, Bible reading, sharing their faith with others, and personal character development.

Today, Layton felt he could tell Craig about his conversation with his father-in-law on the day of Brianne's high school graduation. The insight had taken him a couple of weeks to process. Now his best friend would have a chance to provide additional feedback.

"In a nutshell," Layton summarized, "I've been doing good things for the wrong reason." He paused to take a sip of coffee. "I've provided Brianne with the best prostheses we could afford. I've encouraged her to participate in every activity that I thought would be safe and productive for her. I've pretended to her and my wife that Brianne's disability isn't a problem—won't be a problem—for whatever she wants to pursue."

"Sounds right to me," Craig affirmed. "We've talked through some of your hesitations about her running, for example, not to mention water and snow skiing. So what's the problem?"

Layton's eyes began to tear as he sat his coffee cup on the table. "I want Brianne's life to be normal."

Craig squinted at his friend. "She is normal. She's one of the most normal people I know. She's extremely well adjusted, if you ask me. And it sounds like you are asking me."

Layton shook his head. "No. I'm the one who hasn't been well adjusted. You see, I realized that I haven't accepted the fact that she'll always walk with a slight limp. She'll always have some pain with a new prosthesis. And she will have some limitations on other movements. I'm the one who's been pretending that she has the same body that she had before her amputation.

"Call it survivor's guilt perhaps. She's handled the situation much better than I have. I've wanted to make it up to her when, in fact, I would have taken away from her all the blessings her disability has brought to our family."

Craig rested an elbow on the table. "Say on."

"God has shown us how he wants to take a misfortune and turn it into a fortune. He redeems our brokenness when we ask Him to. Brianne's cancer brought our family back together; it led me to begin my trophy case of trophies of grace; it's given us opportunities to share our faith with others. And Brianne's reaction to her loss has helped other disabled children and adults have confidence in their own wholeness. She's a walking, talking, joy-filled overcomer."

"I see what you mean." Craig paused. "Have you shared this with Amy?"

"Yes. She thinks I'm being too hard on myself. But I'm not telling you this as a confession or to rid myself of guilt. I'm able to say I'm beginning a new walk in the light of God's grace. What He gives is always more than what life takes away."

❧

Layton and Amy stood with the others at the finish line of the half marathon course. Amy held the field glasses, awaiting the first glimpse of Brianne rounding the final curve. As usual, she would cross the line hand in hand with a Special Olympics runner—someone she would have trained to be a part of the annual event.

"I see her!" Amy yelled. She took Layton's arm as they fastened their eyes on their only child. Brianne never intended to finish first or even in the top dozen or so. She aimed to finish with her fellow student, who would be thrilled simply to have completed the race.

"The participation ribbon might as well be covered in gold," Layton observed, as the student by Brianne's side jumped up and down. His parents encircled them, joining in the dance of joy.

Eventually Brianne broke free and came to her parents' side. "We finished with a pretty good time, didn't we? I'm hardly even winded." She sank to her knees and groaned as she rolled over on the soft grass. "Not!"

Her parents laughed with her. "Why, it's only 104 degrees in the shade," Layton teased. "Come on, we're parked close by. I think you need a milkshake."

❧

The summer before Brianne's freshman year of college continued to pass quickly. Mother and daughter had fun shopping for her dorm room with twin beds. Of course, deciding on a color scheme meant working it out with Brianne's roommate, a friend she knew from her high school graduating class.

Although they'd taken a few classes together through the years, they'd hung out with different social groups. Lori Mays had been in the marching band and Spanish club. Brianne knew she was a Christian, although she attended another church in the city.

Brianne felt sure they would get along great. She told her mom, "Lori has a great sense of humor, and she's very responsible. We also have several differences—which should make life interesting."

"Like what?"

"Well, she's used to sharing a room with her younger sister. I've got a lot to learn about sharing my space. She made better grades and loves to read. Maybe my study habits will improve."

"That's a relief," Amy teased. "Maybe you'll even decide on a major."

"I'm in no hurry. Dad says most freshmen take the same classes regardless of their majors. He's letting me take an elective to 'broaden my horizons.'"

"Did he say that?" Her mom laughed. "I can't wait to find out what you came up with."

"Introduction to Sociology," she replied. At her mom's blank look, she added, "The study of the development of human society."

Her mom nodded with that *I don't know where this is going* look that she often wore after talks with her daughter.

"I'm a people person. I wish I had your flair for design." Brianne sighed. "I think I'm more the administrative type."

Her mom gathered her in her arms. "You're on to something. By the time you were four years old, we knew you'd someday take over the world."

❧

Brianne and Ryan Braxton shot baskets in his driveway while Amy and Beth sat on the front porch watching them. "So how do you really feel about your only child living on campus this fall?" Beth asked. She held Ryan's younger sister in her lap. Her second child had been a surprise but a welcomed one at that.

Amy twirled a reddish curl between her fingers. "I'm just trying to soak up every experience I can with my daughter before she leaves home. Belmont is so close to our Green Hills neighborhood that we'll see her often. Nevertheless, we are passing a milestone. I'm excited for her."

"Good. I'm glad you have your business to occupy you. So many mothers dread the last child leaving home." Beth looked down at her two-year-old. "By the time Angela leaves home, I'll go directly to the nursing home."

"Silly." Amy frowned at her friend. She turned her head to watch Brianne make a basket. "I'm sure I'll stay busy. At least I can visit my parents in Miami whenever I choose. There are advantages to being empty nesters."

"Your mom and dad are special. Ryan claims he still has a crush on Meme."

Amy smiled a self-satisfied smile. Having given Brianne so much of herself through the years, it might just be a nice relief to have some time for herself.

Humming to herself, Lori Mays walked from the bathroom into the dorm room she shared with Brianne Brooks. She brushed her wet, dark blonde hair, a robe loosely tied around her. "Brianne, the bathroom's all yours. Time to get up."

Brianne peeked out of her twin bed covers, one eye still shut. "No way." She yawned. "Tell my professor to meet me here. In fact, invite the whole class."

Lori pulled off her sheet and helped her to sit up. "They can't possibly fit in this tiny dorm room. You'll have to go to them." She sat on her twin, still brushing her hair and watching to make sure her roommate didn't fall back on the bed. By this time in the semester, she was accustomed to waking Brianne. Miss Sleepyhead tousled her hair as she stretched.

Lori had grown comfortable seeing Brianne put on and take off her prosthesis. She'd often seen her maneuvering from bed to chair to the doorway without it. This morning, her roommate chose to put it on before heading to the bathroom next door.

Lori followed her into the bathroom. "Do you want to meet for lunch after class? At this rate, you've no time for breakfast."

Brianne attempted an answer, but with toothpaste swishing around in her mouth, the word came out garbled. "I'll take that as a no." Lori grinned. "Meet you back at the dorm later." She headed to their room.

While dressing, Lori patted herself on the back for choosing such a compatible roommate. The two had known each other in high school, but when they discovered they'd both been accepted at Belmont University, they agreed to share a room. Freshmen didn't have an option of off-campus housing, unless they lived at home, and who wanted to live at home?

She'd grown so much spiritually in the past few weeks. At first, Lori had been doubtful that a weeknight Bible study in their dorm room was a good idea. What if she had a test the next day? Brianne had countered that Lori had other places she could study, it only lasted for an hour, and she was under no obligation to be there. "Just make your bed this one night a week," she'd asked.

Lori remembered tossing a throw pillow at her. Was she that careless about her side of the room? Anyway, the Bible study had soon outgrown their room. Now they were meeting in a conference room in the student center. No need to make her bed at all. She grinned at her good fortune.

Walking to the cafeteria, Lori continued to think about the Bible study. Brianne had soon captured the other attendees' interest. Yes, she was a beautiful, petite strawberry blonde. Yes, her humor made every session interesting. Often, she used handouts, Bible maps, and archaeological facts. But mostly, the girls found her credible.

Hearing all that Brianne had gone through in life was sobering to the mostly upper-middle class girls, whose main concerns had been passing grades and talking about boyfriends. Brianne's story had come out in dribbles, mostly in reference to their questions.

Amazingly, she took no credit for what God had accomplished in her life. Like her volunteering with Special Olympics, running in half marathons, and winning swim meets. Lori had been surprised when she captured the coveted title of homecoming queen her senior year with a special needs student as her escort.

According to Brianne, her mission in life was to give God glory. She'd told her Bible study group about her dad's trophy case and the theme of adding trophies of grace. She'd challenged each of them to ask God to show them a character trait they were to build into their lives for His glory. Lori had committed to working on patience.

How fortunate to be Brianne's roommate and get to observe her up close and personal. She was who she appeared to be—but definitely hard to get out of bed in the morning.

"So how come you believe in God?" Alan asked.

"Because I know Him personally." Brianne leaned over and whispered in Alan's ear, "He talks to me often." Then she winked. "And I see Him at work around me every day."

Alan laughed as he gathered the papers they'd been working on for their sociology class. "You're too smart to believe that stuff."

Brianne shot back, "I'm too smart not to believe it." She stood up and shouldered her backpack.

"So where's your proof God exists?"

"Where's your proof God doesn't exist?"

"Oh, come on. You're avoiding the question." Alan followed Brianne to the door.

"It's a fair question, and I'd love to share my proof with you. Call me sometime next week. Right now I'm meeting my parents for lunch." Brianne turned the doorknob.

"But if God exists, aren't you, I mean … mad at Him?"

"About what?" Brianne tilted her head. Soft strawberry-blonde curls fell across one cheek, hiding a bright blue eye.

Alan looked down at her left leg showing beneath her capri pants.

"About my prosthesis? A result of childhood cancer. No, I'm not mad at all. As a matter of fact, God used my first cancer diagnosis to bring my parents back together after a divorce. The second bout with cancer led you to ask me about my faith. You might say this artificial leg is a trophy of God's grace."

As Brianne stepped into her car, Alan gave her a half wave from the doorway. She grinned, wondering if he'd phone her.

She recalled her Meme's counsel when they had talked about her cancer: "Instead of asking God why, ask Him what—what He intends for you to learn through the experience—and what your story might mean to someone else."

She'd thought long and hard about that last statement: what would her story mean to someone else? She made mental notes when friends would ask about her lost limb. A reply took shape that seemed to satisfy believers and unbelievers alike. Both wondered why her strong faith hadn't been enough to heal her without the amputation.

"Look at me," she began. "Do I look healed?" They would nod

their heads in assent. "God chose this method," she said, pointing to her prosthesis, "but He could have chosen other means. This particular answer to prayer caused you to ask about my faith. And I've been able to share my trophy of God's grace."

When answering unbelievers, her response took a little more time. She waited until she felt the Spirit's go-ahead to tell them about God's love, His plan for restoring them to relationship with Him, and His forgiveness. Several had received Christ as Savior because of her testimony.

Brianne started her car and glanced in her rearview mirror. Her new friend Alan still stood on the porch, his hands resting on his hips. Winking at his reflection in her rearview mirror, and for her ears only, she quoted Meme Dyer's favorite expression. "God's up to something."

᪥

Brianne walked into the restaurant where her parents had already taken a table in front of the window. Her mom looked her over, as only moms do, to see how college was treating her daughter.

"You look sweet," she concluded. "Almost as sweet as you smell. What's the new perfume?

She named the familiar brand as she pulled out her chair. Her dad rose to slide it back in place. "Thanks for meeting us downtown for lunch. How did you find a parking place?"

"I walked from the parking garage three blocks away." Brianne placed a napkin in her lap and took a sip of the soft drink her parents had ordered for her.

Layton paused with his drink midair. Would he ever get used to the ease Brianne had in walking on her prosthesis? "I suppose I should be impressed, but the garage is mostly downhill to here."

"Funny, Dad. So, what's the big occasion? You know I'd rather be on campus studying," she teased.

Amy spoke up. "Your dad got a big promotion, that's what." She waited for the news to sink in. "Best of all, he won't be traveling."

"Only when I need or want to," Layton corrected.

"Great, Dad." Brianne looked from one parent to the other. "So you're now president of the company, I assume?"

"No, just a regional manager. I still report to New York's main office."

Amy jumped in, "And now that my little birdie is out of the nest, I get to go with him every time he flies into LaGuardia. Guggenheim Museum, here I come!"

Brianne cocked her head. "I don't know how I like being called a birdie, but I'm glad for you both." She looked at her dad. "If I'm a kitten, don't cats eat birds?"

"Please, not at the table," he said in mock horror. "Let's order." The three ordered the lunch plate special and continued the conversation about her dad's new responsibilities. Then, after their lunch arrived, he asked, "What about you, Kitten, er … Birdie? What have you been up to?"

"I just left Alan Phillip's place. We're doing a research paper together for sociology."

"Whoa …" Amy put up her stop sign hand gesture. "You were at a guy's house? When did that get to be okay with us?"

Brianne sighed. "Mom, it's broad daylight, he's got three roommates, and he knew I had a lunch date with you. I felt pretty sure he wouldn't attack me."

Layton came to her rescue. "So, tell us about this Alan guy."

Brianne lit up at the question. "He's a junior. He's not a Christian. In fact, he doubts there is a God. I'm hoping he'll call me so we can finish our discussion—"

"At another public place," Amy interrupted.

"Wherever. The next move is God's." Brianne started to fork her first bite of meatloaf.

Layton suggested, "Let's pray to that end." The threesome joined hands and bowed to pray as other diners looked on with curiosity.

Several days later, Alan caught up with Brianne on her way to student parking. Out of breath, he leaned against her car. "How's God today?" he asked.

"Why don't you ask Him? He's only a prayer away."

"I thought maybe he calls audibles. Like the quarterback on the football field."

"That too. What can I do for you?"

"I wondered how the sociology paper is coming along."

"I sent you my part on the library computer. Haven't heard anything back from you."

"I've been pretty busy lately. I was thinking if I sent you my stuff, maybe you could write it for me?"

"Not a chance." Brianne stashed her backpack in the passenger seat.

"But it's due next Friday." His gray eyes turned cloudy.

"So it is. You'd better get on it." With that, she started the car. No way would she let him get away with this excuse. After she and Alan had been assigned partners in class, she'd heard from other students he was an ace at getting girls to do his work for him.

Alan leaned in before shutting the car door. "So when are we going to continue that discussion … you know, your proof of God?" Brianne thought over her answer. He didn't come across as a serious seeker after truth. He would no doubt string her along until she went out with him. She decided on a more direct route.

"Why don't you meet me at my church Friday night? We're having a rodeo."

"Sure you are. Don't most churches in Nashville rope cows?"

"Come and see for yourself."

"Okay. How about if I pick you up?"

"I'm on the decorating committee, and you don't want to get there that early." She grabbed a pencil and piece of paper from the front zipper pocket of her backpack. She wrote the name of the church, the address, and the date on the page and handed it to him. "Be there at seven-ish. We're grilling burgers and hot dogs. Come hungry."

With that, she waved a goodbye and inched away from her parking spot. She uttered an audible "God, You take it from here."

<

Intrigued by the idea of a church rodeo, Alan showed up at 7:20 Friday night and parked at the back of the building. Several playing fields and a children's playground occupied grassy acres behind the sanctuary. He followed a line of people heading for a ticket booth in front of a makeshift admission sign. Reluctantly, he grabbed a few bucks from his wallet and bought the fewest number of tickets offered.

Once inside, he followed another line of folks moving toward the outdoor grills and picnic tables. He spotted Brianne wearing a canvas apron, hair pulled back in a ponytail, serving sides at a long table. "Hey, Brianne," he hollered.

She looked up and motioned him over. In her best western drawl, she said, "Have some grub, young feller." She piled a heavy paper plate with coleslaw, baked beans, and potato salad. "Go git yer burger and drink. I'll catch up with ya later."

Alan sat down at a table by a guy who looked to be a college student. The guy ate hurriedly but stopped to introduce himself and shake hands. "Dalton, here. Sorry, man, but I've got to get to the calf-roping booth. Walk around and enjoy yourself." With that, he gathered his disposables and headed off. Alan ate in silence, looking around at the young families and children, while older adults seemed to be in charge of the cleanup.

Once finished, he ambled toward a sign that announced, “Horse Racing.” Men and boys were galloping around a makeshift track on toy horses—the kind you see in a toy store standing in a round barrel. The track had low hurdles and curves to make it more interesting. All the participants were whooping and hollering.

Alan chuckled at how such a gimmicky event seemed fun. Next he approached the calf-roping booth. Sure enough, three tickets bought you three chances at roping a stuffed animal sitting on stacks of hay. A real-life cowboy showed the children how to throw the rope he’d tied. If Alan was correct, someone behind the booth helped the rope to go around the animals. He ducked around back, and sure enough, Dalton winked at him.

Then he came to a pony ride—only the ponies were donkeys borrowed from a farmer’s pen. The farmer guided the donkeys along, gently nudging the animals if they got stubborn. An adult walked beside each bareback rider.

Brianne caught up with Alan at the petting zoo circled with chicken wire. He had to give up the few tickets he’d bought to enter. “Hey,” she greeted him. “Having fun yet?”

“Sho ’nuff, missy,” he drawled. “So tell me, what’s all this about?”

“Oh, this is our church’s fall festival. It’s a fundraiser for our children’s playground. Each year, we try to come up with a different theme.” She put her thumbs in her jean pockets and rocked back and forth as she said, “Guess we were scrapin’ the bottom of the barrel this year.”

Alan couldn’t help but laugh. They stopped to admire baby goats, a few chickens, caged rabbits, and lots of puppies and kittens. Someone from a pet rescue group handled adoption applications. Some baby ducks swam in a children’s blow-up swimming pool, and a cantankerous calf bellowed for all he was worth.

Brianne led him back out and toward a crowd gathering around folding chairs at one of the ballparks. “This year, the college department is in charge of the entertainment. Our youth minister will be speaking in a few minutes. But first, you get to hear the newly formed college country band.”

She motioned him toward a chair, handed him her purse, and announced she’d be back later. “Save me a seat.”

This whole thing is so hokey, Alan thought, but everyone seemed to be enjoying the make-believe rodeo. He sat back in his chair, crossed his ankles, and waited for the show to start.

Soon, the band set up on stage. *It gets worse*, he thought. Band members were dressed in cowboy attire and carried such instruments as a washboard, a harmonica, a fiddle, a banjo, and a big drum. They started warming up in what would have made a newborn nursery sound melodic.

The emcee turned out to be none other than Brianne herself. After welcoming the crowd, she introduced the band with countrified names and gave a commercial straight from a night at the Grand Ole' Opry. Then came the music. Obviously, the players had never in their lives seen the instruments before. Their attempts at playing them, along with serious faces and country dance steps, were hilarious.

To add to the amusement, Brianne announced each song as though it were a real, old-timey hymn: "In the Sweet By-and-By," "I'll Fly Away," and "Victory in Jesus." Alan didn't know the hymns, but he knew the screeching couldn't be right.

After the band left the stage, Brianne gave a heartfelt introduction to the church's youth and college minister, a guy named Brad. He began speaking, and soon Brianne slipped into a seat beside Alan.

"You noticed," Brad said, "there were no pigs in the petting zoo. Pigs are messy creatures. They like nothing better than to roll around in mud. Ever been in a mud fight? Ever come into the kitchen after you've been in a mud fight? Ever heard your mama yell at you like that before?"

The crowd chuckled. "Well, tonight, I'm going to tell you about a guy who'd been in a mud pit with a bunch of pigs. Yeah, that's right. In fact, he was in charge of feedin' the pigs. Do you know what pigs eat? Naw … you don't want to know what pigs eat.

"Anyway, this feller was feedin' pigs when he had a thunderbolt straight from on high. 'What am I doing here feedin' pigs when I'm practically starved to death myself? Why, the hired hands at my father's farm are better fed than me. And they have clothes to wear instead of these rags and a covered place to sleep.'

"But, you see, he didn't think he could go home and apply for a job at his dad's farm. He'd cut his ties with his father, taken what inheritance he would have gotten, and blown the whole thing on a week in Gatlinburg and Pigeon Forge." At this, the audience roared their appreciation.

"Why, he'd ridden the Blazing Fury at Dollywood a dozen times, seen every show in town, visited the Ripley's Museum, played miniature golf, and eaten more chicken and dumplings than a body is allowed. When his money ran out, and after the motel kicked him out, he found this lousy job tending pigs. 'I got nothin' to show for my wild week away,' he cried, 'septin' this half-eaten biscuit from Kentucky Fried Chicken.'

"Then he got an inspiration. 'I'll go home and tell my father I'm not worthy to be nothin' but a hired hand. I won't complain about the pig slop—all I want is a used pair of jeans and a roof over my head when it rains.' The idea so appealed to him that he left right that instant. He hitchhiked all the way back to Nashville, mostly ridin' in the back of pickup trucks 'cause he smelled so bad.

"The last driver let him off at the gate to his dad's farm. He started walking the gravel road to the main house. By now, it was daylight, and he thought he saw someone walking toward him. The image got closer and closer. He shrank back toward the fence line, hoping not to be seen by anyone he knew.

"He could see the image of a man runnin' right toward him. He crouched in the ditch, hands over his head. The man reached down, grabbed him, and pulled him up in an embrace. 'Son, you're home. Wait till I tell yo mama! Let's get you a bath and some clean blue jeans and have us a barbeque.'"

At this, for some reason, the audience started clapping.

Brad stopped and let the crowd settle. "And this, my friend, is the story of you and me and our heavenly Father, who welcomes us into His arms, no matter how much pig slop we got on us."

He led a prayer and exited the stage. The crowd began folding their chairs and taking them to an equipment bus in the parking lot.

Alan turned to Brianne, a puzzled expression on his face. She pulled a slim New Testament from her purse and handed it to him. "Read the story for yourself." Sure enough, she'd marked Luke chapter 15.

Lori plopped onto her bed and took off her sneakers. "Your mom called earlier."

Brianne glanced her way. "I'll call her back in a minute."

Lori fell back on her bed. "It's so hot on campus. And it's almost November. Thanks for getting us a first-floor room. I don't think I could have climbed the stairs."

Brianne tensed. She'd had a lifetime of asking for special accommodations due to her prosthesis. For example, her special parking sticker. Her independent nature rebelled against the idea that she might be limited in what she could do. Feeling that she owed Lori an answer, she remarked, "I could have managed the stairs, but as many times as we come in and out of the dorm each day, I thought—"

"Oh, I totally get it," Lori interrupted, looking embarrassed that she'd called attention to Brianne's disability. Changing the subject, she asked, "What are you reading?"

"Alan's contribution to our sociology report. It's pretty bad."

"Well, if you'd written it for him like he wanted," she drawled the last word, "it would have been much better."

Brianne leaned an elbow on her desk. "Now I get to rewrite it for him."

"Save the original," Lori suggested. "Maybe you can use it as blackmail."

"Good idea." She grinned as she hopped to where the phone hung on the wall. "Better call my mom. She's a worrier." She heard her mom pick up the call. "What's up?" she asked. "If you want me to come for dinner, I'll be right over."

"No way," her mom replied. "We paid for those cafeteria meals, and you're going to eat them whether they're digestible or not."

They laughed. Then Amy continued, "I just had to share my good news with you. Meme and Papa are coming for Thanksgiving. Isn't that wonderful?"

"It's so wonderful! That must mean they're doing well?"

"They're amazing. So far, they've started a Spanish-speaking adult Bible study class at their church, and they have a neighborhood Good News Bible club for the children after school one day a week. On Saturdays, they pack supplies for a food bank for the needy.

"Papa complains about how tired he is when they get home; then he falls asleep in his rocker with the biggest smile on his face. Meme thinks it's all an act."

"I'll call her and let her tell me the news," Brianne said.

"Good idea."

"Right now I'm polishing the sociology paper I'm working on with Alan—you know, that sinister guy who lured me to his house last week for who knows what evil purposes?"

"Now you're making fun of me," her mom grumbled. "I just want you to be careful."

"I am. Brinks Security has asked me for some tips."

"Okay, I'm hanging up now that you've made me feel foolish. I love you, sweetie."

"I love you too, Mom."

❧

Brianne made sure the sociology report had been turned in to the professor in good order before she finally accepted a lunch invitation from Alan. They met at an off-campus Chinese food restaurant. Most of the lunch crowd had left, so the place was relatively quiet.

Alan tried to impress her with his skill at eating with chopsticks. Brianne ate with the obligatory fork, laughing as noodles slid between his fingers. Sipping her hot tea, she withdrew a pad and pencil from her purse. "You wanted to talk about God, right?"

"Yeah. What's with the paper? I didn't know there'd be a pop quiz."

Brianne poised her pencil midair. "I need to know a little bit more about where you're coming from. It's a place to start."

"Whoa. This sounds like a setup."

Brianne took another sip of tea. "It's not. Really. So why are you so interested in hearing my proof for God?"

Alan thought about his response. "In sociology class, our prof said all the ancient cultures worshipped some form of a god. I wondered why. Maybe because they were trying to figure out how they got here on earth. Before science explained it."

"Science has theories. Correct me if I'm wrong, but it has no explanation that it can prove with facts."

He grinned. "Okay, I'll give you that one. But you said you had proof."

"Not so fast. I'm still picking your brain. What is it you think science knows?"

Alan shrugged. "I mostly slept through science classes. Something about a big bang and the origin of the species and a bunch of archeologists time-dating everything."

"So there's no Creator?"

"I think I remember some particle came from some other universe and started the whole process. But you're going to tell me God did it. Right?"

Brianne looked up. "We'll get to that. Next question: where did we come from?"

Alan grinned again. "My folks came to Tennessee from Ohio."

"No, not Ohio. I mean originally. The human race. The Bible says God made mankind from the dust of the earth. What do you think?"

Alan pursed his lips. "Well, a really cute amoeba caught the eye of this other amoeba, and he led her out of the water onto the beach, and—millions of years later—I popped out of my mother's tummy."

Brianne wrote silently. Without looking up, she asked, "And where did the amoeba come from?"

"I don't know. A speck of space dust? There's a lot we don't know about the universe. There may be life forms out there somewhere."

Brianne put down her pencil and folded her arms across her chest. "What's your purpose in life? Your reason for being here? What gets you up in the morning?"

"Do I need a mission statement? Does a cat need a mission? Scaring rats, maybe?"

"Be serious."

"Okay." He paused. "Get a degree. Go into the music publishing business. Make a name for myself. Marry a homecoming queen—er, present company excluded, I guess—have kids, and retire in the Bahamas. Oh, and help little old ladies across the street."

"How noble!" She wrote on the pad. "Next question: what's gone wrong with the world?"

"Who says something's wrong? I'm having the time of my life."

This time, Brianne let out a big sigh. "Surely, you read the paper or listen to the news. Ever hear of Vietnam, or world poverty, or racial protests? What about the murders right here in Nashville?"

"Oh, that kind of wrong. Hey, don't look at me. I've got a clean police record—maybe a couple of driving violations—but what's with that look?"

"Have you ever done anything really bad, Alan? Oh, I don't want to know what. I just want to know why? What caused you to do it?"

"I guess I'm not perfect. Neither are you. What's the next question?

"Fair enough." Brianne picked up her pencil. "What can be done about it?"

"About what?"

"About the evil in the world. About our imperfections."

Alan's expression had turned sullen. "I don't intend to go into politics, ok? Not a lawyer, not a judge, not even a talk show host. Don't look to me to solve the world's problems. I just want to make music, cool music, music to dance to. That should make the world a better place." He crossed his arms with smug assurance.

Brianne kept writing. "Now, last question: what happens when we die?"

Alan sat up straighter. "That's easy. Skeletons buried under six feet of dirt."

Still writing, Brianne asked, "Is that all you are, a bag of bones covered in skin? What about that part of you that makes you unique, the real you? Where does it go?"

"Sorry, Brianne, you only get one shot at life. Like my dog, Penny. When she's gone, she's gone. Nada. Nothing."

The waiter brought their checks and fortune cookies. Alan read his. "*You will find a new hobby*. Interesting. I didn't know I had an old one. I'll be on the lookout."

Brianne read hers. *"Wisdom is the sum total of life experiences."* She commented, "Only if you draw the right conclusions from them." She finished her hot tea and cleared her throat. "Now, if I may recap your pop quiz."

She had his full attention. "You're not sure where the universe or people came from, but the question doesn't seem to bother you. Your purpose for life is admittedly self-centered. You hope to live a comfortable life with a family and a job you enjoy.

"As for what's wrong with the world, you don't think it's your fault or yours to fix. You're pretty satisfied that you're one of the good guys, although you mess up at times. As for what happens when you die, you've observed that dead people leave skeletal remains. That's it. End of Alan Phillips."

Alan thought over her words. "Seems a little cold. I don't think I'm different from any of my friends. Now, if you want to meet some really bad dudes, I can take you down to—"

"No, thanks," she interrupted. "That was just a quick summary. Fair enough?"

"Fair enough. My turn now? I get to ask the questions?"

Brianne placed her elbows on the table and stared into his gray eyes. "I'm not putting you off, but I've got a class in twenty minutes. Think about your answers, Alan. Is that all you want out of life? Is that enough to keep you going if—heaven forbid—bad times come your way? If life lets you down? Is this a viewpoint that will instill in your kids the values you hope they'll develop? Will it keep your wife faithful or the music flowing? What if you're wrong?"

Alan lowered his eyes. "I need to be going too. Catch up with you later." With that, they gathered their things and walked toward their separate cars.

"See ya," Brianne called. Alan kept walking.

Several days later, Alan heard a voice mail from Brianne on his dorm phone: "Meet me in the student center when you can. I'll be studying for midterms." He didn't want to appear too eager, although she was definitely the prettiest girl on campus. And hard to catch.

So far, only a handful of guys had garnered a date, and only one of them had made the cut for a second one. None of them seemed to care about her prosthesis. She was popular. Maybe it had become something of a game to see if she'd go out with you.

He'd had time to mull over his responses to her questions about his beliefs—or assumptions. He supposed he knew how she'd answer the same questions, but curiosity is a cruel master. He grinned.

Around four in the afternoon, he ambled into the student center just to grab a soda and happened to catch her eye. "Oh, hi, Brianne. I got your message. What's up?" He pulled out a chair at her table and held his drink on his crossed knee.

She closed her book. "Have you thought any more about your answers to my questions the other day?"

He took a swig of his drink. "Yeah. Don't know anything I'd change. Maybe add a few more details about dead bodies."

"That's okay. I think I get it. My biology lab was yesterday. So, I suppose you'd like to know how I'd answer the questions I asked you?"

Alan tilted his head, curiosity getting the best of his better judgment. "I think I know pretty much how you Christians think, but go ahead."

Brianne turned somber. "This is not my answer to how I know there's a God."

"I guess that means we'll have to get together a few more times? Maybe some evening at a downtown music venue. I pick you up—"

"Or maybe you'd better wait to hear my answers."

Alan grinned. "Okay. Game on." He sat his soft drink on the table and leaned in. "I remember question one: where did the universe come from?"

Brianne replied, "I'll try to keep it brief, but here goes. I believe the universe is too orderly, the laws of nature too exact, for the world to have accidentally or haphazardly come into existence. Thus, I believe in a Creator who spoke the world into existence and created everything that we see around us."

"Where's your evidence?" Alan chided.

"Did you present any evidence? I remember only theories. You never explained how an unconscious bang or blob produced consciousness. Next?"

"Fine. Where did we—human beings—come from?"

"The Bible says God created man from gathering dust from the ground. In other words, man came from particles that He'd already created. Then He formed woman out of man's rib. All original materials. No hocus-pocus."

Brianne paused. "I've got to tell you this joke. A man told God he could create life. God accepted his challenge. The man reached down and collected a handful of dirt. 'Wait,' God said. 'You have to use your own ingredients.'"

Alan grinned. Brianne continued, "Everything came from somewhere or something. I believe the most logical origin is a Creator."

Alan cocked his head. "Next: what are we doing here?"

"We're here to give glory to God. Glory is a word that refers to brilliant light. We're to shine a light on who God is and all God has done for us. We do that by placing priority on a personal relationship with Him and caring for each other and His creation."

Alan frowned. "So what does that have to do with getting a college degree? Sounds a little abstract to me."

"God shows us our place in the world over time. He leads us and guides our choices. His plan is for us to have a life full of purpose. That life varies according to our abilities, personalities, likes, and dislikes. Keep going." She waved her hand at him.

"All right. What is wrong with the world?" Under his breath, Alan muttered the quip, "You and I are the only sane people left, and sometimes I worry about you."

Brianne chuckled, then turned somber. "The first humans were not willing to obey God's instructions. Basically, they wanted self-rule. When they disobeyed, sin corrupted the world and everything in it. Now humankind knew good from evil. God allowed them the freedom to choose. However, choosing evil would result in dire consequences. Since then, we all choose sin."

"Sin? I thought the devil made me do it." Alan smirked in triumph.

"The devil," she continued, "encourages rebellion in us, just as he rebelled against God. But we choose sin because our inherited nature is to want to be our own god."

Alan looked down at his crisscrossed fingers. "So sin is the problem. What exactly is sin? I mean besides murder, lying, robbing—"

"You're quoting from the Ten Commandments, which God gave to Moses." She winked at him. "Thanks for proving my point. Sin is missing the mark. Not hitting the target. Messing up your life and the lives of others by not living according to how God made us to function. He is the Inventor. Maybe we should pay attention to His instructions?"

"So I'm a sinner. I bet you are too. What can be done about it?"

Brianne answered. "We—you and I—can't do anything about ridding our world of sin. Sure, we can do good deeds, help the poor, work for justice. People have tried that for centuries. But the sin problem won't go away. God had to intervene in order to rebuild the relationship with Him that sin had broken.

"At just the right time in history, God sent His Son, Jesus, to earth as the God-Man to provide the perfect, sinless sacrifice for our sins. His death on the cross conquered sin, death, and hell. By accepting His sacrifice as payment for our sins, we have a restored relationship with God. GRACE is God's Righteousness At Christ's Expense. A holy God relates to us through the lens of Christ's sinless perfection."

"That's a little much to take in all at once." Alan uncrossed his knee and scooted up to the table. "So, God likes us now. Bottom line: what's in it for us?"

"We have the very Spirit of God living within us to guide and encourage our journey toward Christlikeness. Bonus? We're assured of eternal life in heaven with God when we die."

"Is this the part about hell?" Alan asked. "I've been waiting to hear this."

Brianne sighed. "Rejecting God's sin sacrifice means there's no other payment for our rebellion against God's rightful place as Lord of our lives. Hell is separation from God. Hell is spending eternity with everyone who has rejected God. Hell is a choice—just as heaven is a choice. Why would anyone choose hell?"

"That's just what Christians believe," Alan countered. "Have you ever heard of the other world religions? How do you know you are right?"

Brianne tilted her head to one side. "That's a worthy discussion. Most of the adherents of Islam, Buddhism, Hinduism, and others are sincere and believe in the truth of their religion. Here's my quick response: religion is mankind seeking God. Its adherents teach us what to do to please a god or gods.

"Christianity is God seeking man. The Bible is the story of God's efforts to reach us. Instead of teaching us to depend on good works for salvation, it tells us we can't save ourselves. Only God can save us when we trust that His Son rids us of our sin debt."

Alan glanced at his watch. He was growing uncomfortable. "Let's finish up. Where do we go when we die?" He sat back in his chair. "I think you've already answered that. You think we either go to heaven or hell. But why? Why not just let death be the end of it?"

Brianne leaned forward. "Because God never intended for us to live seventy years, be beset with illness and suffering and loss, and then wither away into nothingness. He intended us to live forever, without death and disease or loss or tears. Death wasn't His original plan for us. Jesus defeated death by rising from the grave. He promised us that we too will rise on the Last Day and join Him in heaven where God reigns eternally.

"If you don't accept God's rule on earth, you're certainly not going to want to spend eternity with Him," she continued. "I'm sorry some people choose not to believe in Him. That's why I so want you to hear this good news." She pulled a sheet of paper out of her backpack. "I wrote my answers for you. Here, take this." She handed him the paper. They rose from the table and gathered their disposables.

On the way out of the building, Brianne asked, "Ready to hear my proof?

Alan shrugged, "Why not? About that date I mentioned—"

"I'll see you in sociology next week. We'll make a plan then. Good luck on your midterms." With that, she turned toward her dorm.

Midterm exams over, Brianne realized how few weeks were left before Thanksgiving. She and Lori were both going to their homes for the holidays. The idea of sleeping in their own bigger beds—and as late as possible—appealed to both.

As they discussed their plans for the holiday, Lori asked, "Do you think I could meet your grandmother while she's in town? I'm very intrigued with your stories about Meme Dyer."

"We'll work out a time when she gets here," Brianne promised. "I'm sure she'll want to meet the roommate I've talked so much about."

Lori's ears perked up. "And what did you tell her about this roommate?"

"I told her you speak fluent Spanish and would love to converse with her."

"No!" Lori shrieked. "Two years of high school Spanish and almost one semester of college Spanish? Fluent? You've got to be kidding."

"Actually, I am," she admitted. "I told her you were the nicest, kindest, most considerate roomie a gal could ever have."

"Whew!" Lori winked. "At least you got that right." They grabbed their backpacks and headed across campus.

൭

On Monday before the Thanksgiving break, Alan stopped Brianne on the way out of their sociology class. They chatted for a few minutes before Alan asked, "About that evidence you owe me? About how you know God exists?"

Brianne turned inquisitive eyes toward him. "Yes?"

"I could give you my undivided attention tomorrow night. The Able Brothers are playing at the Bluebird Cafe in Green Hills. How about I pick you up—"

"And we listen to a band play for an hour? Doesn't sound like undivided attention to me." Alan thought over his options, which seemed pretty clearly in her favor.

She tilted her head as she thought about an alternative. "Let's go to the Pancake Pantry in Hillsboro Village. If we go between the breakfast and lunch crowd, it won't be so busy. The place doesn't play loud music, and eating pancakes puts me in a great mood."

Alan agreed to meet her at ten the next morning. He headed for his next class, wondering if he could dig up any evidence to support his case between now and then.

૭

Tuesday morning turned out to be a perfect autumn day in Nashville. Brianne drove the few blocks to the Pancake Pantry, wishing she had time to walk. She uttered another audible. "God, You've given me this opportunity. I trust Your Spirit with the outcome."

Alan, seated at a back table, waved at her. The service was good, and the pancakes arrived in the middle of their chitchat.

"So, why are you taking sociology?" Brianne asked. "I haven't heard a thing about music publishing all semester."

"It's an elective," he replied, scooping a mouthful of pecan pancakes. "I figure if I'm going to work with different kinds of music from different backgrounds, I might get some good clues about cultures, stuff like that. What about you?"

Brianne grabbed a napkin and dabbed at the blueberry syrup dribbling down her chin. "An elective for me also. I don't have a declared major yet. Sounded interesting."

The discussion soon turned to Thanksgiving plans. Alan said, "I'll be in Cookeville at my parents' place, just hanging out. Probably see a bunch of high school friends, most of whom go to Tennessee Tech and are still living at home."

"Why didn't you do that?" Brianne asked between bites.

"My major—and the chance to live in the big city of Nashville." He laughed. "For a small-town guy, this is as good as it gets."

"So, what will you do with your friends?"

"Oh, play touch football, catch up with each other. Tell lies about how well we're doing with our studies."

Brianne grinned as she scraped the last of her syrup off the plate. "Got a girl back home?"

"Did. Past tense. She went to UT in Knoxville. Marie's family is spending the holiday in Pigeon Forge."

She put her elbows on the table and leaned in. Alan took the cue. He carefully folded his napkin and nodded her way. "I'm all ears." Just then, a waitress came by, cleared the table, and left a check. "I've got this," Alan said as he took the piece of paper. "I asked for this conversation."

She sat up straight and began, "How do I know there's a God? I could answer that question many different ways. There's nature itself. The Bible book of Romans says people have seen the earth and sky and all that God made. They have no excuse for not knowing God. That's Romans 1:20. I mentioned earlier the order of the universe. I could add the amazing diversity of animals and the human body that evolution can't explain. But that's not my answer.

"I could mention the consistency of the biblical record. Did you know that the Bible was written by approximately forty men over sixteen hundred years and numerous civilizations and doesn't contradict itself? These writers didn't know each other or speak the same language. Yet the Bible is seamless in its story. In the Old Testament, forty-four prophecies about Jesus came true. I could also mention all the archeological evidence for people and places mentioned in the Bible. I'm not going there either.

"I could lean on my own personal experiences with God. How I've found Him to be true to the characteristics He claimed for Himself in Exodus 34:6–7. He's kind, compassionate, slow to anger, loving, and forgiving. He spared me from an early death and healed me in His own good way, brought my parents back together after a divorce, and blessed me with a Christ-focused home. I have God's very Spirit living inside me because I trusted Jesus as my Savior and gave Him my heart and soul. But if I said that, I'd be sharing my experience, which only proves my faith works for me."

Brianne paused and took a sip of her fresh coffee, which the waitress had just refilled.

Alan waited, then said, "So, I'm glad you didn't give me the ole' time religion. My parents took me to church occasionally. I know about Noah and the ark, David and the giant, and Daniel in the lion's den. I know Jesus did miracles and healings and taught good things. But other faiths have their holy books and sacred rituals. Those I've met from other countries seem to be good people. Bad people are found in every faith tradition, even in Christianity. Look at the martyrs burned at the stake by other Christians." He sat back in the booth, a satisfied smile on his face. "So, what else you got?"

"I've got you."

"Me?" Alan exploded. "I'm your evidence?"

"Yes. I believe you are my proof God exists."

Thanksgiving break turned into Thanksgiving Day. In keeping with southern tradition, everyone at the Brooks' house left the table stuffed like the forlorn turkey. The family gathered in the living room to watch televised football. The ladies talked softly among themselves. Papa's head began to nod while Layton carried on a one-way conversation with the referees.

Soon, the doorbell rang. "That's probably Lori," Brianne exclaimed and rose to answer the door.

Lori entered, shedding her coat and scarf. "Hi, everyone," she shouted over the football noise.

Layton turned down the volume and stood to take her things. Brianne guided her to where Meme sat in her favorite armchair. "Meme, meet my roommate, Lori Mays. Lori, this is Jan Dyer."

Meme rose to gather Lori in her arms. "Just call me Meme. I'd love to have another granddaughter. Especially one who speaks fluent Spanish."

Lori gave Brianne a frantic look. Brianne grinned. "Meme is in on the joke. Don't worry." A relieved Lori hugged Meme, then Amy, and sat in a side chair across from mother and daughter, who nestled on the couch.

Layton announced he was heading for his man cave. "I know better than to watch my football game in a hen house. If Papa wakes up, send him back with me." He took off.

Meme carried on an animated conversation with Lori, putting the young lady at ease. When the conversation lapsed, Lori turned to Brianne. "Have you told them about your conversation with Alan?" Then she turned to the others, "It's the most amazing story I've heard in a long time."

Amy turned to her guest. "You are referring to Alan Phillips, right?" When Lori nodded, Amy continued. "Brianne mentioned that she'd gotten to witness to him about the Lord." She looked at her daughter. "Is there more to the story?"

Brianne cocked her head. "Well, more detail. We haven't had a chance to sit and talk much since I came home. Something about cooking and baking—"

"Well, the big meal is over," her mom announced. "We eat leftovers for the next three days."

Meme said she wanted to hear the whole thing—whatever they were talking about—right from the beginning. Lori settled back in her chair and crossed her legs, ready to listen to the retelling.

Brianne began with Alan's initial question about why she believed in God. "He thought, if there is a God, I should be mad at Him about my leg." She grinned at her grandmother. They'd been over this subject at length.

"So," she continued, "I asked him if we could begin by comparing our beliefs—so I'd know his point of view. That took a while. Basically he doubts a Creator and assumes death is the end of existence. Life's purpose, for him, is to produce music and have a few comforts along the way."

Her mom shook her head. "Sounds like the message our culture shouts to us every day. 'Eat, drink, and be merry, for tomorrow we die.'"

Meme nodded. "So sad. He's on his own in a vast universe, competing with everyone else for every crumb. How does he make value judgments and moral choices if he's his own highest authority?" She lowered her eyes to her lap.

Her mom asked, "So what happened next?"

"I let him think about his vantage point. Then, days later, I felt led to present my viewpoint."

Meme sat up straight in her chair. "He didn't have any evidence to disprove God. I hope you told him his were just theories."

"I did. But, despite the proof from nature, the Bible, history, and archeology, belief in God is ultimately a faith proposition. God apparently didn't intend for facts to convince us. He wants a love relationship with us instead."

"Great answer," her mom exclaimed. "So what did you say is your evidence then?"

Lori exclaimed, "What Brianne said was brilliant."

Brianne brushed off the compliment. "Alan. Alan is my evidence."

Lori jumped in. "This next part is really good."

***

Brianne suggested she get them each a glass of tea. The movement gave her an opportunity to think again about the conversation between Alan and her at the Pancake Pantry. She reviewed in her mind what had been said between them.

"Let me backtrack a little," Brianne had begun. "Do you remember that I said Christianity is God seeking mankind, not mankind seeking God?"

Alan nodded. "I'm still not sure what that means."

"The creation account in the Bible describes God creating man and then woman in His own image. He talked to them in the Garden of Eden. He confronted them when they disobeyed him. When they discovered they were naked, He clothed them.

"The Bible doesn't say, 'Man and woman sat around one day and wondered if maybe there is a God somewhere. Then they thought up what He'd be like and what His rules might be and wrote it in a book.

"Do you see the difference? God sought relationship with His created beings, told them the rules for living in the garden, and punished them when they disobeyed. Like a loving Father.

"He continued to seek out their descendants. First Noah, then Abraham, then the children of Jacob—called the Israelites—and then Moses. None of these went looking for God. God showed Himself to them. He spoke to the prophets. And finally, He revealed Himself through His Son, Jesus Christ."

"Okay, I get it." Alan leaned back in his chair. "Supposing all these Bible stories are true. God seeks a relationship with us. But why? What's in it for Him?"

Brianne pulled a Bible from her backpack and looked up John 3:16 and read: "'For God loved the world in this way: He gave His One and Only Son, so that everyone who believes in Him will not perish but have eternal life.'" She turned a few pages over and said, "When Jesus prayed for the disciples before His crucifixion, He asked His Father to affirm His love for us." She read from John 17:23: "'May they be made completely one, so the world may know You have sent Me and have loved them as You have loved Me.'"

She turned a few more pages. "John wrote after Jesus's death and resurrection: 'Look how great a love the Father has given us, that we should be called God's children.' That's 1 John 3:1."

She gave Alan a pointed look. "That's why God redeemed us, Alan. He wants a love relationship with us. Not one commanded or enticed by personal favors. Not one based on perfect daily choices. One based on the choice to return His love."

Alan sipped his coffee, obviously thinking about what she'd said. Finally, he picked up Brianne's copy of the Bible and held it up. "Fine. God loves us and wants us to love Him. That's what the Good Book says. But what does that have to do with me? You said I am your evidence for God."

Brianne signaled the waitress for another warm-up for her coffee. "Alan, since the age of nine, people have asked me what happened to my leg. Most accept my answer that God chose to heal my cancer through amputation.

"In your case, you not only asked about my prosthesis, but you continued to question my reasoning. You've pursued the issue right up until this very minute."

"So, I'm curious. What does that prove?"

"It proves God is drawing you to Himself." She turned to John 6:44 and read: 'No one can come to Me unless the Father who sent Me draws him.'

"You see, Alan, I'm not the one who excited your curiosity. It wasn't my well-crafted answers to your questions or my witty comebacks. God is at work in your life, and I'm just the person watering the seed. He does the rest."

Alan grew uncomfortable under her steady gaze. "How do you know I won't just drop the subject once we leave this place?"

"I don't know. But, then, convincing you to believe in God is not my job." Brianne folded her arms on the table. "Have you ever heard of the poem 'The Hound of Heaven' by Francis Thompson?"

Alan shook his head no.

"The author describes running away from God—hiding, hoping not to be found. Instead, God pursues Him. God is like a hunting dog after His prey. Thompson concludes that God is after his love and won't leave him alone.

"If you can resist God's love, Alan, you can write the sequel to

Thompson's famous poem. But you will have missed the greatest gift this world has ever known." Brianne flipped the Bible's pages to Romans 8:35, 38–39 and read:

> Who can separate us
> from the love of Christ? …
> For I am persuaded that neither death
> nor life,
> nor angels nor rulers,
> nor things present, nor things to come,
> nor powers,
> nor height, nor depth, nor any other
> created thing
> will have the power to separate us
> from the love of God that is in Christ Jesus
> our Lord!

Brianne put her Bible back in her backpack, zipped it up, and stood.

"You're leaving?" Alan asked.

"Yes. Remember, you're paying." She grinned. "But I'm not leaving you alone. You've got the actual hound of heaven right behind you."

Then she walked away.

ꕥ

The ladies were staring at Brianne as she remained lost in thought. "Sorry," she said, delivering the tea glasses. She sat back on the couch beside her mother.

"What happened after you told Alan he was your proof of God?" her grandmother asked.

Gladly, Brianne told the rest of the unfinished story. She sighed. "I hope that's not the end of Alan's curiosity, but it's really up to his heavenly Father to continue the pursuit."

Meme's bright blue eyes sparkled. "I believe God is up to something."

Brianne had only been back on campus a few days when Alan approached her in the cafeteria. "Hi," he said. He sat down at the table she occupied with Lori. Lori quickly excused herself and headed to the tray return station.

"Hi, yourself." She cocked her head. "How was your holiday?"

"Good. A little change of plans." He smiled.

"Oh, really? No touch football—or was it lying about your grades?"

"Actually, neither. You may remember I mentioned a girl I'd dated in high school? Marie? She's attending UT in Knoxville. I didn't expect to see her over the holidays."

"Yeah?"

"As it worked out, her younger brother came down with the flu. Her family didn't go to Pigeon Forge for the holidays after all."

"Bummer," Brianne said—then, noting his expression, took the words back. "I mean, good. Sorry for him but apparently good for you two."

"We talked a lot."

Brianne gave him a big smile. "I'm guessing you're pleased about that."

"Yes. Next semester, Marie is transferring back to Tennessee Tech in my hometown. She didn't prefer the big city and big school. Guess I'll be going home a lot more on weekends."

"Way to go." She extended her hand and gave him a high five.

"Here's the kicker," he continued. Alan looked around them as though he would be telling a big secret. "It seems Marie has a roommate who got her started in a campus group that holds Bible studies."

Brianne lifted her eyebrows.

"Yeah, and now Marie—she's, she's different. She said she gave her heart to Jesus—whatever that means." He nervously searched his fingers folded on the table. "I didn't tell her about our talks. I guess I was too blown away by her talking about religion."

"Religion—or Christianity?" Brianne questioned. "You know there's a difference."

"Yeah, right. I'll check your notes," he said. "Anyway, I've got to be running. Just wanted you to know." Alan gave her a mock salute and headed for the exit.

Miraculously, Lori appeared from nowhere and hurried to take her former place at the table. "I'm all ears," she announced. "What did Alan say?"

~

"Well, hello, Meme." Brianne leaned a blue-jeaned leg against the wall of her dorm room. "Your ears must have been burning."

Meme didn't miss a beat. "I wondered why my ears felt hot. I guess you're going to tell me."

"No," Brianne teased. "First, you're going to tell me why you called."

"I just wanted to make sure I had your roommate's last name spelled correctly. I wanted to drop her a note thanking her for stopping by to see me while we were at your house for Thanksgiving. I so enjoyed our conversation. I couldn't remember what kind of 'maze' she is."

"It's M-A-Y-S," Brianne replied. "That's so sweet of you."

"Well, if it hadn't been for her, I might never have heard the story about your friend Alan. I've been praying for him ever since. Now, why are my ears burning?"

"Because earlier today, Lori M-A-Y-S and I were talking about that very same conversation."

"Oh really? What brought that up?"

Brianne proceeded to tell her grandmother about Alan's news. "Now you can update your prayer requests to include Marie."

"Sure thing. I'm adding Marie to the list as we speak."

"Yes. Pray that her new faith will grow once she's back in her hometown—away from the influence of her Christian roommate."

"I have it on good authority," Meme responded, "that the hound of heaven will be hot on her heels." Brianne could feel—if not see—her Meme's warm smile. "Keep me posted."

"I will," Brianne promised. "I am so fortunate to have a praying grandmother. Not everyone here on campus is so lucky."

Meme cleared her throat, the way she always did when she was commended. "Then let's just have a prayer together right now."

ꟹ

The Christmas holidays came and went without any drama. When Brianne's semester grades came in the mail, she immediately called Lori to compare her results.

"You beat me, as usual," Brianne complained. "I hoped your good study habits would rub off on me."

"Hey, you passed everything, didn't you?" she quipped. "You were involved in more campus activities and led a Bible study, not to mention all your church activities."

"You're just trying to make me feel better." Brianne moaned. "I guess I'm not the sharpest pencil in the box."

"You're plenty sharp, Brianne. You just have different priorities. I'd love to have your personality—your way with people. You are a natural when it comes to making others feel at ease around you."

Brianne thought about Lori's response. "Well, if you're trying to make me feel better, you succeeded." The young women talked about when they would be back on campus.

Lori asked about her classes. "I hope you're not taking a second semester of sociology. I don't think I can stand the excitement of another of your class assignments."

"No," she replied. "This semester it's Introduction to Psychology."

"Here we go again." Lori groaned. "Who will God team you up with this time?"

ꟹ

Amy took off her shoes and massaged her aching toes. Layton looked down at her as he tied his tie in front of the bathroom mirror. "You must have been on your feet all day. What were you up to while I sat in boring meetings?"

Amy padded to the window in her stocking feet and pulled the curtain back. "New York, New York. Too much to do. Not enough time."

Layton grabbed his jacket and joined her as they looked down at the traffic streaming through the Lincoln Tunnel. "I guess I could carry you down to dinner?" He gave his wife a peck on the cheek.

"No way. But I'm tempted." She padded back to her discarded shoes, slipped into them, and grabbed her jacket. They exited their hotel room and rode the elevator to the main-floor dining room.

After they were seated at a table looking out on the busy street, they opened their menus and selected different options. Layton folded his napkin on his lap. "Are you surprised we haven't heard from your little chickadee?"

"Birdie," Amy corrected him. "Not really. She's back in school for the semester and probably neck deep in assignments."

"It is unusual that she hasn't checked in with us, don't you think?"

Amy reached for his hand. "I think she knows this is the first out-of-town trip we've taken without her. She wants us to just enjoy each other's company."

"Hmm," Layton mused. "Why do you think that?"

"Because it's the last thing I said to her before we left home."

Her husband chuckled and held her hand tighter. "Sounds like you've moved into the empty nester phase of life at last."

Amy dusted imaginary feathers from her lap. "I'm resting in the assurance of God's tender care for my birdie. We've done what we can to lay a firm faith foundation. I believe Brianne can take it from here."

EPILOGUE

Brianne Brooks straightened her graduation robe and mortarboard. Lori Mays stood beside her as they waited to line up for the march into the graduation venue. Lori's engagement ring sparkled in the midmorning sunlight.

"Too bad you're not already married," Brianne teased. "You'd at least be able to sit with us Bs."

"Ah, Mrs. Roger Burton. I like the sound of it. But, then, I wouldn't still be your roommate." She checked her watch. "At least for the next three hours or so."

Tears began to flow. The two young women clung to each other until the order to line up separated them. Brianne took her place, still thinking about Lori's upcoming wedding and move to North Carolina, where Roger would enroll in a master's degree program.

Brianne would stay put, getting a master in business administration. Moving back home would be difficult. The three Brooks had worked out an agreement that would allow her some independence. Now, she needed a job.

The line began to move forward into the building. Brianne looked back, but Lori was hidden from view.

❧

Layton Brooks looked on with pride as his daughter marched across the stage at her second graduation ceremony—unaware of the slight limp in her step. She proudly accepted her diploma from the Belmont University chancellor and took her place in the graduate seating area.

Craig Braxton, sitting on one side of her father, punched his shoulder and gave him a wink. Layton winked back.

Yes, he remembered the ah-ha moments that followed Brianne's high school graduation. He'd wished she hadn't limped—until, of course, Papa Dyer had reminded him that the limp was a sign of God's trophy of grace.

Layton looked down the row of family to where Papa sat. He wondered if Papa remembered the conversation that had set him to thinking about how God had redeemed her suffering.

In fact, Layton and Amy had carried on a similar conversation that morning as they were getting dressed. He'd voiced his pride in Brianne's college years. "She's special, just like her mother."

Amy had turned to him, her brilliant blue eyes sparkling. "I remember, after her amputation, asking God to show me the fruit of His plan for Brianne, why she had to suffer so much. Through the years, I've seen that fruit displayed in many ways.

"Meme was so right," Amy continued. "She said, 'He's saving her life for some good purpose. You just wait and see. God's up to something.' And He was."

READER'S GUIDE

Use these questions for personal reflection or group study:

1. Describe Layton's game plan for the Christian life? Was it working for him?
2. React to Layton's thought that prayer resembles "pulling the emergency brake while parked on a steep hill. You might not need the extra precaution, but then again—you might."
3. Myra said, "Suffering is an equal-opportunity employer." Have you found this to be true?
4. Why did Amy call her mother a beam of hope?
5. Do you agree with Myra that "You can choose your feelings"?
6. Layton said, "We think He should be taking care of every situation so we don't have to go through stuff. Really, He's here to go through stuff with us." Give an example.
7. Myra told Layton after Claire's funeral, "Sorrow shared is divided in half." Do you agree?
8. What do you think the author meant by "letting silence do its work of grace where no words dared intrude"? How can you apply this truism?
9. React: "Some memories aren't worth the trip back to retrieve them."
10. Meme told Brianne, "Your dad was a lost sheep, and we knew the Shepherd." How would you have reacted in a similar situation?
11. Explain Meme's counsel to Brianne, "Instead of asking God why, ask Him what."
12. Meme said, "Christ is called the Redeemer because He's busy trading the bad for the good." Give a personal example.

13. Layton asserted, “I’m beginning a new walk in the light of God’s grace. What He gives is always more than what life takes away.” Do you agree?
14. What did you think of Brianne’s approach to presenting her proof to Alan that God exists?
15. Brianne said, “God apparently didn’t intend for facts to convince us. He wants a love relationship with us instead.” What difference would “salvation by facts” have made?
16. Share how the hound of heaven pursued you.
17. As you think about death, how has Myra’s testimony influenced you?
18. What role did forgiveness play in this story?
19. What was God’s good purpose in healing Brianne?
20. Who was your favorite character?

MEET THE AUTHOR

Dr. Betty Hassler loves translating her forty years as a pastor's wife into true-to-life stories of families growing in their faith despite life's difficulties.

Betty is an accomplished speaker, writer, and author of both nonfiction and fiction titles. She has cowritten nine Bible studies and numerous articles for Christian publications. With seventeen years of experience in Christian publishing, she served as editor of two magazines with a combined distribution of a million readers.

Betty has a bachelor of arts degree in English from Baylor University and a master's and PhD degrees from Southwestern Baptist Theological Seminary. She has served on church and association staffs and as a Christian counselor.

Now as a freelance editor and writer, she lives with her husband and near her two sons and grandchildren in northwest Florida. She loves practicing conversational English with international students and traveling.

Coming Soon from WestBow Press

A Stash *of* Faith

Trophies of Grace Series

BOOK 2

Turn the page for a preview of Chapter One.

Spring 1989

Dr. Parker Sloan Hamilton had no warning that today would be the worst day of his life.

With a cup of freshly brewed coffee in one hand and the *Miami Herald* in the other, he opened the sliding glass door to the balcony of his high-rise apartment. In the distance waves splashed the sandy beach. The beginnings of morning traffic snaked along the coastline.

Settling into his wicker deck chair, he placed the cup on a marbled table and unfolded the newspaper. Blazoned across the bottom half of the front page, a picture stared back at him. Recognizing the face immediately, Parker's pulse quickened. Dino DiMarco had been one of his high-profile facial makeovers.

The article told that a suspect had been caught in a murder for hire scheme. Of course, the name DiMarco appeared nowhere in the story. Other people in the makeover business handled the details of providing new identities and documents for his patients. Parker had only been responsible for creating the new faces.

The cops would still be able to trace DiMarco's real identity through fingerprints. Parker could do nothing about that. What if he or someone else turned state's evidence and identified him as the surgeon? What if the district attorney decided to prosecute him? The what-if 's made his stomach churn.

Parker hurriedly dressed and drove to work. As he entered the county medical examiner's office, the irony of his workplace wasn't lost on him. He was one of their lead forensic specialists.

Valerie waved from her cubicle. "Hi, Parker, how's it going?" The every-morning ritual grated on his nerves this particular day. He nodded and kept going. At six-feet four-inches tall, he supposed it would be hard to sneak quietly to his desk. Being voted most eligible bachelor in the mock office pool hadn't helped obscure him. That embarrassing distinction might soon be coming to an end.

Once at his desk, he listened intently to the office chatter that always preceded his workday. Would the DiMarco story make the morning conversation? He felt exposed, as though any coworker passing by would see guilt written all over him.

Trying to distract his thoughts, he checked his e-mail. Who'd been brought in during the night and now awaited his attention on a cold slab in the morgue? The work—gruesome to most of his friends—intrigued him. Now the dark cloud hanging above him left a growing sense of foreboding about his future.

Midday Parker complained to his supervisor of a migraine and begged off early. He drove home in a heavy rainstorm, downed several pills, and waited. For what? He wasn't sure.

ஒ

South Florida had been a far cry from Boston, where Parker had completed his training in forensic pathology. He'd soon adjusted to the culture, if not to the heat. The laid-back mañana philosophy contrasted sharply with his duties in the county medical examiner's office, where identifying victims and the nature of their deaths was more than a full-time vocation. Bodies were discovered at all times of the day and night.

Although he loved the excitement of his work, Parker had missed the connection to facial reconstruction that had drawn him to the field of forensic medicine. To scratch that itch he'd become friends with several cosmetic surgeons in the area. Occasionally, he found himself in a consulting role, particularly when a well-known celebrity flew in for a makeover.

One friend in particular, Dr. Brody Colson, had been more than understanding of his need for a few prescription drugs to make it through the day and to relieve his chronic insomnia. He also let him in on a trade secret.

"The rich and famous aren't the only ones coming to us for cosmetic surgery," he told Parker. "Some people want to look different for other reasons. Maybe they don't want to be found. They want to disappear for awhile and reappear with a new identity." Brody winked, but Parker stared at him in disbelief.

It seemed clear Brody implied these were people with a criminal past or present. They were trying to evade the very law enforcement agencies with whom Parker worked.

Brody continued, "I know what you make in the medical examiner's office. And I know your lifestyle. Soon the two are going to collide. This service pays well. Very well."

Brody was right about finding it hard to live on his meager paycheck. Having grown up in a wealthy Nashville neighborhood, he'd taken the finer things in life for granted. But that was no excuse for engaging in an illicit activity. Parker had reasoned that he could pick up extra income at any area clinics or hospitals. Except for his crazy hours. How could he even schedule a part-time position?

Parker had the random thought of blowing the whistle on the criminal makeovers, but he decided to keep quiet. Brody knew about his drug habit. That wouldn't look good to his supervisor. He thought consulting on a new look for a few patients was his best option for a little extra cash.

That decision led to assisting with surgeries. Finally, he performed his first solo surgery on a person wanting a makeover. Uncomfortable with the success of the procedure, Parker told himself he' d never do it again. For the hundredth time, he weighed his options.

Operating on individuals wanted by law enforcement might be risky behavior, but it was lucrative. And he craved Brody's admiration of his skills. He was solving crimes in the medical examiner's office while moonlighting by surgically altering faces. What irony! To Parker, the nameless criminals were simply limp figures on a gurney attached to an IV tube.

At the time, Parker had wondered what his father would say about the questionable nature of his side job. More than likely, Hollister Hamilton would care more about the potential damage to his own social status and reputation if Parker were caught. As a partner in a prestigious Nashville law firm, Hollister had a certain image to maintain—one that had always superseded concern for his son.

❧

The pills subdued his headache but not the anxiety. Parker waited for his phone, the doorbell, the security desk—some sound to confirm his worst fears. Had he really thought he could get away with surgery on criminals who had lots of money but few places to hide?

Was it too late for him to run?

Printed in the United States
by Baker & Taylor Publisher Services